A BOOK OF
OGRES AND TROLLS

A BOOK OF
OGRES AND TROLLS

by
Ruth Manning-Sanders

ILLUSTRATED BY
ROBIN JACQUES

E. P. DUTTON & CO., INC.   NEW YORK

First published in the U.S.A. 1973 by E. P. Dutton & Co.

Copyright © 1972 by Ruth Manning-Sanders

LIBRARY OF CONGRESS CATALOGING IN PUBLICATION DATA

Manning-Sanders, Ruth, 1895—   A book of ogres and trolls.

SUMMARY: Thirteen traditional tales from several countries
recount the exploits of a variety of ogres and trolls.

1. Tales.   [1. Trolls—Fiction.   2. Folklore]
I. Jacques, Robin, illus.   II. Title.
PZ8.1.M298Bn   398.2'1   73-77454   ISBN 0-525-26998-3

Printed in the U.S.A.
First Edition

Contents

Foreword

W hat is the difference between an ogre and a troll? To begin with, ogres all are all huge creatures, and trolls, though they are sometimes very big, are just as often very little, like dwarfs. The ogres usually live in castles; the trolls make their homes in caves, or in grassy mounds, and they live in the northern parts of the world, in Iceland, Norway and Denmark. You will not find a troll venturing south, nor will you find an ogre going very far north; for ogres and trolls never live in the same countries.

On the whole, too, trolls have the pleasanter natures. True, they have their own peculiar way of looking at things, and they can be very mischievous; but they can also be very kind – provided always that you deserve kindness. But woe betide you if you don't treat them with respect!

Take, for instance, the Icelandic story *Tritil, Litil, and the Birds.* Here you will find the trolls' characteristics, both of body and mind, very clearly shown. The troll wife is an enormous creature; but Tritil and Litil are tiny and dwarflike. Tritil and Litil are kindness itself to the good lad Kurt, and the troll wife really loves him (though it amuses her to pretend she doesn't); but neither Tritil nor Litil nor the troll wife will stand any nonsense from Kurt's impertinent brothers.

You will meet with another lavishly generous and affectionate

7

troll in the story *Jon and the Troll Wife*, also from Iceland.

Two more stories from Iceland, *The Gold Knob* and *Sigurd the King's Son*, give us other troll characteristics. The troll Kidmus in *The Gold Knob* is a mischievous fellow who likes his joke, but he is not wicked. And the troll wife in *Sigurd the King's Son*, threatening though she may seem, has under it all an affectionate nature. But nothing good can be said of Father Troll in the same story. Nor perhaps of the troll in the Danish story *The Troll's Little Daughter*, who is, however, more pathetic than wicked. As to the troll wife in yet another Icelandic story, *Cow Bu-cola*, she is a thief, and to turn her into stone is the best that can be done for her.

Coming now to ogres. A *good* ogre is such a rarity that the Russian story in which he appears has to be called after him. In fact, as far as I know, he is the only really pleasant ogre in existence. The ogre in *The Children on the Pillar* (another Russian story) is a horror; so is the ogress in the Sicilian story *The Green Bird*; so also is the ogress in the Italian story *The Girl in the Basket*. All the ogres in *The Little Tailor and the Three Dogs* (a story from Germany) are wicked, cruel and treacherous. And the ogre in another Sicilian story, *The Ogre's Breath*, is a very tiresome fellow, giving a lot of unnecessary trouble.

So here, in this book of stories about ogres and trolls, we have once more the familiar fairy tale mixture: good and bad, kind and cruel, stupid and clever, cunning and straight, with the hero or heroine having a really tough time of it; but, with courage and perseverance, they triumph over all their troubles, and bring themselves, and us, to rejoice together in a happy ending.

1. The Good Ogre

There was once a widow who had an only son, a lad called Durak. Folk said that Durak was a simpleton; but simpleton or no, his mother couldn't afford to keep him. So, like other lads, he had to go out into the world to seek for work.

So he walked along, and he walked along, and he came to a mountain. At the foot of the mountain was a great cave, and at the entrance to the cave sat an ogre. And that ogre was huge enough and ugly enough to make a body faint with terror at the sight of him: his great eyes rolled in his head like fiery wheels; his great body was covered with bristles, and his great flat scaly feet had claws on them instead of toes.

Now Durak's mother had told Durak that when he went out into the world he must mind and be polite to everybody he met. And this was the very first body that Durak *had* met; so he off with his hat and made his best bow. 'Good day, sir,' says he, 'I hope I find you in good health this morning? Can you kindly tell me how far it is to the place where I wish to go?'

The ogre opened his great mouth and let out a blast of laughter that blew Durak heels over head. 'Mannikin,' said the ogre, 'what are you called, and where do you wish to go?'

Durak picked himself up, dusted his hat, put it back on his head, took it off again, made another bow, and said, 'Mother calls me Durak, sir, for I am not overwise; and Durak, so I've heard tell, is the name of a fool. And the place I wish to go to is the place where I can find work.'

'Will you work for me?' says the ogre.

'Gladly, sir,' says Durak.

'And what about wages?' says the ogre.

'Would a penny a year be too much?' says Durak.

At this the ogre roared with laughter again, and Durak fell down again, and picked himself up again, and dusted his hat again, and bowed again. And the ogre said, 'A penny a year will suit *me* all right. I have a herd of cows for you to look after, and mornings and evenings you must make me a bowl of porridge. That's all I live on, milk and porridge. I have a delicate digestion,' said he with a sigh.

So Durak lived with the ogre and worked for him. It was an easy and pleasant life. He liked sauntering out with the cows to their pasture in the dewy morning, and sauntering back to the cave with them in the evenings. And though at first he burned the ogre's porridge every time he made it, the ogre was patient with him, and he learned better by and by.

And at the end of the first year the ogre gave Durak his penny.

'Will you work for me another year, Durak?'

'Yes,' says Durak.

That morning, when Durak drove the cows to pasture he stopped at the ogre's well. What did he do then? He took his penny out of his pocket and threw it into the well. 'If that penny doesn't sink,' says he, 'I shall know that I have served my master truly.'

But the penny sank.

'There!' says Durak. 'That's because I burned the porridge.' And he shook his head and walked on after the cows.

Well, Durak lived for a second year with the ogre, and the days went peacefully by. At the end of the second year he got his second penny. What did he do with it? He threw it into the well after the first one. The penny sank. 'There!' says he. 'That's because I let my master's fire out once or twice.'

So he worked for the ogre yet another year, and at the end of this third year, the ogre took a gold coin out of his left ear and gave it to Durak. 'I'm raising your wages, my boy,' says he.

But no, Durak wouldn't take the gold coin; he wanted his penny, and he got it. He went to the well and threw this third penny into the water. What happened? The penny floated, and the other two pennies rose to the surface of the water, and floated with the third one.

'Oh ho!' says Durak. 'Now I have truly served my master!'

And he scooped all three pennies out of the well and put them in his pocket.

'Durak,' says the ogre next morning, 'it's time you left me and went to seek your fortune.'

'Is it, master?'

'Yes, Durak.'

'Well, as you say, master.'

'Here's a bag of food for you,' says the ogre.

'Thank you, master,' says Durak, and slings the bag over his shoulder. Then he said goodbye to the ogre, and wandered off into the world.

He walked along, and he walked along, and by and by he felt hungry. So he sat down and ate up all the food he was carrying in his bag. Then he got up and walked on again. And he hadn't gone very far when he met an old woman who said she was starving.

'Well then,' says Durak, 'buy yourself some bread.' And he gave her his first penny.

So he walked along, and he walked along, and by and by he met an old beggar man, and he was starving too. So Durak gave the beggar man his second penny, and said, 'Buy yourself some bread.'

All day he wandered on. He didn't know where he was going; but, bless me, that didn't trouble him! In the evening he came to the sea shore, and on the shore was a little ruined hut. 'I will live in this hut,' thinks he. And he went in, curled up on the floor, and fell asleep.

Now there was a seaport near by, and there were boats coming and going. Durak found work among the boats, loading and unloading, and earned a penny or two to buy bread. And a man gave him a fishing line and some hooks, and showed him how to bait the hooks and set the line along the sand at low water. And of the fish he caught, Durak ate some, and gave the rest away to anyone who asked for them. So he lived, and never gave a thought to what the ogre had said about seeking his fortune. But though he didn't seek it, yet his fortune came to him, as you shall hear.

One day there was a great stir in the seaport. Bakers, butchers, grocery men and fruiterers were scurrying to and fro about the quay, loading provisions into a big ship. The ship belonged to a merchant, who stood on the quay, checking up the goods that were brought to the ship.

Durak went as close as he could get to the ship, and gazed at it in admiration. 'That's a fine vessel, your honour,' says he to the merchant. 'Would your honour be sailing far in her?'

'To the ends of the earth to seek my fortune,' says the merchant. He looked at Durak and laughed. 'Would you like to invest in my venture?'

'Why not?' says Durak. And he gave the merchant his third penny, which all this time he had kept wrapped up in a handkerchief.

The merchant set sail. He arrived in a foreign port; he sold his goods, made a handsome profit and was about to return home again, when he remembered Durak's penny. 'Must buy the poor fool something,' he thought. And seeing a lad who was teasing a big tabby cat, he gave the lad Durak's penny and took the cat.

Then he set sail for home. But a great storm arose, the merchant's ship was blown this way and that way. He was in danger of foundering when he saw an island ahead, and a port with a fine harbour – though what island and what harbour it was, he hadn't a notion. However he managed to steer his ship into the harbour, and there he waited until the storm had blown over.

Now the island belonged to a duke, who lived in a palace overlooking the harbour. And the Duke, who loved company and got but little of it, invited the merchant to take supper and spend the night with him. It was a very grand supper, but the merchant had never felt less inclined to eat; for there were big rats running all over the table, and servants stood behind each chair, beating off the rats with sticks.

After supper the duke showed the merchant to his room for the night.

There was no bed in the room, only a great chest with air holes pierced in the lid. 'Yes', sighed the duke, 'we all have to sleep in chests, because of the rats.'

'But haven't you any cats?' said the merchant.

'Cats?' said the duke. 'What are those?'

'I'll show you,' says the merchant. And he went to his ship and fetched the big tabby cat which he had bought with Durak's penny.

'You can take the chest away,' says he to the duke. 'I'll sleep on the floor with the cat.'

'But the rats will kill and eat you!' cried the duke.

'Not they!' said the merchant.

Well, there it was, since the merchant wouldn't sleep in the chest, the duke went away and left him – and lay awake all night, thinking to find nothing of his guest but some gnawed bones in the morning. But in the morning – what did he see? The floor of his guest's room strewn with dead rats, the merchant curled up in his cloak, sound asleep, and the sleeping cat curled up beside him.

'Three times its weight in gold!' cried the duke. 'I'll give you three times its weight in gold for that animal!'

So the merchant got the gold, and the duke got the cat; and the storm having blown itself out, the merchant set sail for home. And when he reached his home port, there was Durak standing on the quay.

'Welcome home, your honour!' says Durak, taking off his hat and bowing. 'I hope your honour made your honour's fortune?'

'Well, not exactly,' says the merchant. 'But I traded your penny.'

'Ha!' says Durak. 'That's good news!'

Now the merchant didn't want to give Durak the big bag of gold he'd got for the cat. He thought he had better use for the gold than Durak had. So he fetched a large flat stone that was part of the ship's ballast. 'Here's what I've got for you,' said he. And he gave Durak the stone.

Durak was delighted. He dragged the stone back to his little hut, made four legs out of driftwood, and set the stone up as a table. 'Now I shall eat my dinner in fine style!' thinks he. And he kindled a fire in the hearth, and set about cooking some fish he had caught. But when the fish was cooked and he brought it to the table – what did he see? His stone had turned into solid gold!

Durak didn't stop to eat his fish. He lifted the table off its legs, and hurried with it back to the merchant. 'Sir,' said he, 'you made a mistake, you have given me too much – take it back!'

Then the merchant was frightened. He remembered he had heard tell that fools were precious to God. 'My son,' said he, 'I have sinned, and heaven has justly rebuked me. With your penny I bought a cat. I sold the cat for a bagful of gold – here, take the gold, take it!' And he handed the bag of gold to Durak, and made him keep the table also.

Durak went back to his hut. What was he to do with the bag of gold? He hadn't a notion. It worried him. It kept him awake at night. For the first time in his life he felt unhappy. And at last he carried the bag of gold down the sand and flung it into the sea.

But, bless me, if the sea didn't wash it in again!

'You'll not get over me that way!' says Durak. And he took the bag into the town, meaning to drop it off the end of the quay into deep water.

At the quayside there was a new ship unloading her cargo. The cargo smelled very sweet. Durak asked the captain what it was.

'Incense,' said the captain.

'What's that for?' says Durak.

'Well, you burn it,' says the captain. 'It makes a sweet smell.'

'It smells sweet already,' says Durak.

'Ah, but sweeter when burned,' says the captain.

'I'd like to smell it burning, then,' said Durak. And he bought the whole cargo of incense with his bag of gold, and carried it off, sackful by sackful, on to the sand in the front of his hut.

'There's a fine pile!' says he.

And he set fire to it.

The scent of the burning incense spread far and wide. The fragrant smoke was drifted by the wind to the ogre's cave. *Sniff, sniff, sniff!* 'What's that lad Durak up to now?' thought the ogre. And he put on his seven-leagued boots and was outside Durak's hut in a twinkling.

'Durak, my son,' says he, 'what are you doing?'

So Durak tells him the whole story, and the ogre laughs and says, 'What *you* want, my lad, is a clever wife.'

'I should like that,' says Durak. 'But where to find her?'

'See that little rock out there in the water?' says the ogre.

'Yes, I see it.'

'Well, you wade out and stand on it,' says the ogre. 'Watch the fishes swim past. When you see one with a gold ring round its neck, catch it up in your hands and bring it ashore.'

'Why?' says Durak.

'Because I tell you to,' says the ogre.

So Durak waded out to the rock, and looked down into the water. Fishes swam by, fishes of all colours – red, blue, silver, brown, and grey, speckled, and striped. And at last came one with a gold ring round its neck; and Durak caught it up between his hands and brought it ashore.

'Now I have a pretty fish,' said he. 'But no wife.'

Oh ho, hadn't he? The fish gave a jump out of his two hands. And there at his side stood a beautiful maiden, with a gold ring on her finger.

'I am to be your wife, Durak,' says the maiden.

Was Durak delighted? I tell you he was! The maiden took him by the hand and led him up the beach. 'Don't look round at the sea till I tell you,' said she.

'Why not?' says Durak.

'Because I say you mustn't,' said the maiden.

'Well, I won't then,' said Durak.

So, when they came near the top of the beach, the maiden said, '*Now* look round, Durak!'

Durak looked round. What did he see? He saw a team of horses, and then a flock of sheep, and then a herd of cows, led by a great bull, all wading out of the water and moving up the beach, orderly as you please.

'Oh ho!' says Durak. 'Whose are those?'

'They're ours,' says the maiden. 'Yours and mine, Durak.'

'Oh!' says Durak. 'Oh!'

'Well then, just you keep your eye on them,' says the maiden· 'And don't you look landward till I say so.'

Durak stood still, and kept his eye on the flocks and herds. He thought he must be dreaming.

'*Now* look to land, Durak!' cried the maiden.

Durak turned round and looked to the land. What did he see? Where his ruined hut had stood amid a tangle of reeds – there, in a pretty garden, stood a cosy little farmhouse with barns and stables. Behind the farmhouse were fields and meadows, and flowing through the meadows was a stream, bordered by willows.

'Oh ho!' says Durak. 'Whose house is that?'

'It's ours,' said the maiden. 'And tomorrow is our wedding day.'

So next day Durak and the maiden were married. The ogre put on his seven-leagued boots and fetched Durak's mother to the wedding. The maiden baked a cake, but the ogre couldn't eat any of it, because of his delicate digestion. So the maiden made him some porridge. She poured cream on the porridge, and the ogre gobbled it up. He said it was the best porridge ever he'd tasted.

2. Tritil, Litil, and the Birds

You must know that there was a king and a queen and a young princess, and one morning the young princess vanished. Yes, just like that – first she was there, and then she wasn't there.

Well then of course the whole kingdom was in an uproar; everyone, from the richest duke to the poorest ploughman, running about searching for the princess; because whosoever found her was to be made the king's heir, and also to marry the princess, provided he wasn't married already. But could they find her? No, they couldn't.

Now there was a farmer who had three stalwart sons; and these sons wanted to go and look for the princess. But the farmer said, 'Yes, you may go, but you must go one at a time, for there's much work to be done here in the fields, and I can't spare the three of you.'

So the eldest son set out. His mother gave him a big bag of food, for the way might be long. His father gave him a stout cudgel, for the way might be dangerous. And he went, went, went, till he came to a grassy mound, and there he sat down to rest and eat.

So, as he was eating, out of the mound stepped a tiny, tiny troll man, *very* tiny, very ugly.

'Give me some of your food!' said the tiny troll man.

'Be off with you!' cried the lad. And he chased that tiny troll man back into the mound with his cudgel.

So, when the lad had eaten his fill, he got up and walked on. He went, went, went, and came to another grassy mound, and there he sat down to rest and eat. And out of the mound stepped another little troll man, even smaller and uglier than the first one.

'Give me to eat!' says the tiny, tiny troll man.

'Be off with you!' cried the lad, and chased the tiny troll man back into the mound with his cudgel. Then he got up and walked on.

He went, went, went, and came into a forest; and in a forest glade he sat down to eat. And there came a flock of birds and surrounded him; and if those birds could speak they were asking for food, and if they couldn't speak, they were still asking.

'Be off with you!' shouted the lad. And he banged with his cudgel on the ground, and hit out with it this way and that way, till all the birds flew off.

Then he got up and walked on. He went, went, went, and in the evening he came to a great cliff. There was a big cave in the cliff, and the lad went in. It was all dark inside, and the lad was groping round, to find a comfortable place to lie down and sleep, when far away at the back of the cave he heard the lowing of cattle.

'That's mighty queer!' thinks he. And it was queerer still when the back wall of the cave opened; and through the wall stepped a monstrous troll wife, carrying a lantern.

'What are you doing here?' bellowed the troll wife.

The lad said he was looking for a place to sleep, for he had come a long way and was weary. And the troll wife said, 'Well, you can sleep here, but you must do me a job of work in the morning.'

'I'll do that,' says the lad. And now he saw that there was a great bed in the cave, piled up with pillows and blankets. And the troll

21

wife heaved herself into the bed, pulled the blankets up over her, and went to sleep. The lad had to lie on the ground, and slept but ill, being kept awake by the troll wife's tremendous snoring.

So, early in the morning, when he had just fallen into a deep sleep through sheer weariness, he was suddenly awakened by the troll wife, who had him by the shoulders and was jerking him on to his feet.

'Time for that job of work,' she shouted. And she walked him to the back of the cave, which opened and let them through into a great shed full of cattle. Beyond the shed there were meadows, stretching as far as eye could see. The troll wife drove the cattle into the meadows, and gave the lad a spade and a rake.

'Now clean out the shed,' she bellowed, and off with her after the cattle.

The lad watched her going farther and farther away, and getting smaller and smaller. And when she seemed no bigger than a bush in the distance, and the cattle were mere specks, he took up the spade to begin clearing the soiled straw from the floor of the shed.

Did you ever? The spade stuck to the floor; nor could the lad move it. He tugged at that spade, and he tugged at that spade till the sweat ran off him; but no, he couldn't move it. So he gave it a kick, and took up the rake. But – bless me! – if that rake didn't stick to the floor also! All day he was tugging first at the spade and then at the rake, but he might as well have been tugging at the floor itself, for neither spade nor rake could he move. So in the evening when the troll wife came back with the cattle, the shed floor was no cleaner than when she had left it in the morning.

'What! Not done!' she roared.

'Of course it isn't done,' says the lad. 'How could you expect it to be done? You've played a trick on me!'

'Yes,' says she, 'and I'll play you another!' And she picked him up, carried him into the cave, and gave him a smack. What happened? He turned into a moth-eaten fur slipper, and she tossed the slipper under her bed. . . .

Back at the farm the lad's two brothers and his father and mother waited, waited. But of course the lad didn't come home. So at last the second son said, 'Father, let me also set out. If I can't find the princess, I may perhaps find my brother.'

The farmer said, 'Yes, go, go!' He gave the lad a stout cudgel, and his mother gave him a big bag of food, and he set out.

And as it happened to the first brother, so it happened to the second one. He came to the first grassy mound, and sat down to eat. The tiny troll man asked him for food, and he chased that tiny troll man away with his cudgel. He came to the second grassy mound, and the second tiny troll man asked for food, and got chased away with the lad's cudgel. He came into the forest glade and sat down to eat; the birds gathered hungrily round him, and he chased them away. He came to the troll wife's cave, and there he spent the night. In the morning the troll wife bade him clean out the cattle shed. But the spade stuck to the ground, the rake stuck to the ground, the lad couldn't clean the shed, the troll wife picked him up, carried him back into the cave, gave him a smack, turned him into a moth-eaten slipper, and tossed him under her bed.

So now there were two brothers who never came home.

The farmer moped, the mother shed tears. 'Father,' said the youngest brother, whose name was Kurt, 'I keep thinking of my two brothers. I don't care a rap about finding the princess – there are plenty of stout fellows searching the world for her. But who is to search for my two brothers, except myself? Father, let me go!'

And the farmer said, 'Go lad!' He gave Kurt a stout cudgel, and Kurt's mother gave him a big bag of food, and Kurt set out.

He went, went, went, till he came to the grassy mound. 'I think my brothers must have rested here,' said Kurt to himself, 'and so will I.' And he sat down and opened his food bag.

Well, he hadn't taken but one mouthful, when out of the mound stepped the tiny, tiny troll man.

'I'm hungry,' whimpered the tiny, tiny troll man.

'Sit down by me then, and help yourself,' says Kurt. 'Here's bread, and cheese, and beer.'

The tiny, tiny troll man sat down by Kurt, and they ate and drank together till they were full. Then the tiny, tiny troll man got up.

'Thank you, friend Kurt,' says he. 'My name is Tritil – call me if ever you find yourself in need.' And he pattered away back into the mound.

Kurt set off again. He walked long, long, long. He came to the second grassy mound. 'I think my brothers rested here,' thought he, 'and so will I.' And he sat down and opened his food bag.

Then out of the mound stepped the second tiny troll man, and said, 'Give me to eat!'

'Sit down by me and help yourself,' says Kurt. 'Here's bread, and cheese, and beer.'

The tiny, tiny troll man sat down by Kurt, and they ate and drank together. Then the tiny, tiny troll man got up. 'Thank you, friend Kurt,' said he. 'My name is Litil – if you ever are in difficulty call me.'

And he ran off into the mound.

Kurt slung his bag over his shoulder, picked up his cudgel, and walked on. He walked long, long, until he came into the forest glade.

'Surely my brothers must have rested here,' thought he, 'and so will I.' And he sat down, opened his food bag, and began to eat.

Then down from the trees flew a great flock of birds. They stood round Kurt and watched him. And if those birds could speak, they were asking for food; and if they didn't speak, they were still asking.

'Here you are then, little fellows!' says Kurt. And he crumbled up all that was left of his bread and cheese, and scattered it round him for the birds.

The birds pecked up every crumb, every morsel. And then one of them spoke up and said, 'Thank you, friend Kurt. If ever you find yourself in need, call us. Say "Come, my birds" and we will come.'

Then all the birds flew away, and Kurt got up and walked on. He walked far, far, and at sunset came to the troll wife's cave, and went in, and heard beyond the back of the cave the lowing of cattle.

'Anyone at home?' he shouted.

Then the back of the cave opened, and out came the huge troll wife, carrying a lantern. 'What do you want?' she bellowed.

'Just to lie down and sleep till morning, if you please ma'am,' says Kurt, 'for I have come very far and I am weary.'

'Yes, you may lie down and sleep here,' roared the troll wife. 'But you must do a job of work for me in the morning to pay for your night's lodging.'

'I'll do that willingly,' said Kurt.

Then the troll wife got into her great bed and rolled herself up in the blankets. But let her snore as loud as she would, she didn't keep Kurt awake. And all that roused him in the morning was the troll wife gripping his arm and jerking him on to his feet.

'Time to get up,' roared the troll wife. 'Have you any food in your bag?'

'No,' said Kurt. 'I gave the last of it to some birds in the forest.'

'Those who waste food must go hungry,' shouted the troll wife.

But, all the same, she brought him a bowl of porridge.

So, when he had eaten: 'Now, for the job of work,' said she.

She took him through the back wall of the cave and into the cattle shed. She drove out the cattle, and gave Kurt a spade and a rake.

'Clean out all this mess before I come back,' says she.

And off she went with the cattle.

Kurt took up the spade to begin his work. What happened? The spade stuck fast to the floor. He left the spade sticking, and took up the rake. What happened? The rake stuck to the floor. Let him tug, let him push, let him heave as he would, neither rake nor spade could he move.

'Oh dear Tritil!' called Kurt then. 'If you can hear me, come!'

And scarcely were the words out of his mouth when tiny, tiny Tritil was standing at his side.

'What's to do here?' says tiny, tiny Tritil.

Kurt told him, and Tritil put his finger on the spade handle.

'Dig, you spade,' says he.

And the spade began to dig.

Then Tritil put his finger on the rake handle and said, 'Rake, you rake!'

And the rake began to rake.

Now the dirty straw was moving out of the shed at a fine rate. The spade didn't stop digging, nor did the rake stop raking, till the floor was clean as a new pin. Then troll Tritil laughed and ran off; and Kurt went out to sit in the sun till the sun set, and the troll wife came back with the cattle.

'Is the job done,' says she, 'that you sit there idle?'

'Yes, it's done,' says Kurt. 'You go and look.'

The troll wife went into the shed and looked. She came out of the shed laughing.

'Lad, lad,' says she, 'you are not alone in this! But I'll let it pass. Only you must stop another night, for I've another task for you in the morning.'

So, when she had bedded down the cattle, she took Kurt under her arm, and carried him back into the cave. She gave him a bowl of porridge, and then they both lay down to sleep, she in the great bed, and he on the cave floor.

In the morning, long before sunrise, there she was, jerking Kurt on to his feet. 'Up with you, clever!' roars she. 'Here's your porridge. And when you've had breakfast, you must carry my bedding out and air it. Take all the feathers out of my three pillow-cases, spread the feathers in the sun, air them well, put them back, and sew up the cases. Here's needle, cotton, scissors, all you'll want. But mind, if there's one single feather missing when I bring the cattle home, it's off with your head and into my pot with you – head, body, blood, brains and all.'

And away she tramped through the back wall of the cave.

Kurt took the blankets off the great bed, dragged them out, and spread them on the grass in front of the cave. The sun was bright, there was not a breath of wind. He went back for the pillows, carried them out, unpicked the stitches in the pillow-cases, and shook the feathers out over the grass. Oh me – what happened then? There came a mighty wind, and there were all the feathers rising into the air and whirling this way and that way. And there was Kurt running about, snatching at handfuls of feathers, stuffing them back into the pillow-cases – only to have them blown out again, and the pillow-cases themselves like live things, flapping round his head.

'Dear Tritil, dear Litil, and all my birds, help help!' he cried.

They were all coming – Tritil and Litil scampering on their little legs, the birds flying fast, each one with a beak full of feathers. They soon had all three pillow-cases full again; and Tritil and Litil sat down cross-legged, and sewed up the cases.

'Here you are, my lad,' says Tritil. 'And here are three feathers we've left out. If the troll wife misses them – push them up her nose. And when she says 'What wages?' you must ask her for three things. *First* – what's under the bed. *Second* – the little chest beside the bed. *Third* – what's through the door on the right wall of the cave. Goodbye to you, Kurt, my lad!'

Hey presto! Before ever Kurt had time to thank them, they were gone – Tritil, Litil, and all the birds. And Kurt carried the blankets and the pillows back into the cave, and laid them tidily on the great bed.

In the evening back comes the troll wife. She stamps into the cave and throws herself down on the bed with such a thump that the whole cave quivers. She takes up the pillows in her great hands and feels them over inch by inch. 'There is one feather missing in each pillow!' she roars. 'So now, my lad, I am going to kill you!'

But Kurt jumped on to the bed, shouted, 'Here you are!' and stuffed the three feathers up her nose.

The troll wife let out a roar of laughter. 'You're not alone in this, lad, lad!' said she. 'But I'll let it pass. Only you must stop here another night, and in the morning you shall choose your wages.'

So they slept through the night; she in the great bed, he on the floor.

And in the morning the troll wife said, 'Now for your wages. You can ask three things, one for each night you have been here.'

'Then the first thing I ask for,' says Kurt, 'is what lies under your bed.'

'Lad, lad, you are not alone in this!' says the troll wife. 'But I'll let it pass.' And she put her hand under the bed and dragged out three moth-eaten fur slippers.

She gave a pat to the first slipper. What happened? The fur slipper disappeared, and there stood a beautiful princess – the very princess that all the world was searching for.

She gave a pat to the second slipper. What happened? The fur slipper disappeared, and there stood Kurt's elder brother.

She gave a pat to the third slipper. What happened? The fur slipper disappeared, and there stood Kurt's second brother.

The two brothers gave one terrified look at the troll wife, and rushed out of the cave, and off home with them, fast as their legs would carry them. But the princess stood there quietly in the cave, and smiled at Kurt.

'Well,' said the troll wife, 'and what next will you be asking for?'

'The little chest beside the bed, if you please, ma'am,' says Kurt.

'Lad, lad, you are not alone in this,' says the troll wife, and she handed Kurt the chest. Kurt opened it. It was full to the brim with gold and jewels.

'The third asking is the last asking,' says the troll wife.

'And I'm asking for what's behind that door in the right hand side of the cave,' says Kurt.

'Oh lad, lad, you are not alone in this!' laughed the troll wife. 'But there, we must let it pass.'

Now Kurt couldn't see any door at all in the right hand side of the cave. He had merely repeated what Tritil had told him to say. But the troll wife strode to the wall and banged on it; and the wall opened. Kurt took the little chest under one arm, gave his other hand to the princess, and together they followed the troll wife through the wall.

What did they see? What did they not see! They saw a splendid ship with a silver hull, and ivory masts, and sails of purple and gold.

'Aren't you the luckiest lad in all the world!' said the troll wife. 'For this ship will sail over the land and over the sea, and carry you wherever you want to go. So – all aboard!'

Kurt put the little chest into the ship, handed in the princess, and got in himself. 'Ship, my ship, carry the princess home!' he said.

And the ship glided away with them.

The troll wife stood to watch them go. A big tear rolled out of one big eye and trickled down her big cheek. 'I could have turned him into a slipper and kept him,' she said, 'But there, what's the good of an old fur slipper?'

That's the end of the story: except to say that of course Kurt married the princess; and after the wedding sailed with her in the ship to visit his father and mother. He gave them the little chest, and all the gold and jewels; and so sailed back again to the king's court, and lived with his princess happily ever after.

3. The Ogre's Breath

One day a young princess was sitting at an open window in the king's palace, when an ogre passed by. What did that ogre do? He drew in his breath, and his drawn-in breath lifted the princess from her chair, and carried her out of the window. And the ogre took her in his arms and strode off with her.

The queen, her mother, fainted. The king, her father, tore his hair. The ladies-in-waiting screamed. The lords-in-waiting brandished their swords and shouted. But the ogre had gone, and the princess had gone, and fainting and tearing of hair and screaming and shouting and brandishing of swords wasn't going to bring the princess back again. So then the king sent out heralds: 'Anyone who can rescue the princess shall have her to wife and become heir to the throne.'

Now in that kingdom there lived an honest labourer who had seven stalwart sons. And each son at his christening had been given a special gift by a good fairy. The eldest son grew to be so strong and swift of foot that he could take up ten men in his arms and run with them faster than the wind. The second son was so keen of hearing that he had only to put his ear to the ground to hear all that was happening in any part of the world. The third, with one blow of his fist, could smash down seven iron doors. The fourth was so clever a thief that he could steal the ring off your finger, or the coat off your back, without your noticing it. The fifth had but to stamp his foot to make any kind of building he wished spring up where his foot had trodden. The sixth had a crossbow with which he could shoot and kill whatever the eye saw, whether near or far, whether on sea or on land or in the air. And the seventh had a guitar whose music would raise the dead to life.

And one day the eldest of these lads said, 'Brothers, what are these gifts of ours worth, if with their aid we cannot rescue the king's daughter? Come, let us set about it!'

'Yes, let us set about it!' cried all the brothers.

So the second brother put his ear to the ground and listened.

'I hear the princess weeping, shut up in a castle with seven iron doors,' said he. 'And I hear the ogre snoring close beside her.'

Then the first brother took the other six up in his arms, and ran with them faster than the wind to the ogre's castle. The third brother, with one blow of his fist, smashed down the seven iron doors, and they all tiptoed into the castle. What did they see? They saw the princess seated on a golden stool, weeping, weeping. And they saw the ogre sprawled with his head on the princess's knees, sound asleep, and snoring, snoring.

Then the fourth brother – the clever thief – stooped over the princess. Hey presto! He had her in his arms, and the ogre's head was resting on a silken cushion. The ogre never stirred, but sprawled with his head on the cushion, snoring, snoring.

So the first brother caught up all his six brothers, together with the princess, and off with him, swifter than the wind. But there was a horrid little dwarf, who was the ogre's servant; and that dwarf, who had hidden himself in one of the ogre's seven-leagued boots in terror of the third brother's fist, now climbed out of the

boot and tweaked the ogre's nose. 'Wake up! wake up!' he squealed. 'Your bride is stolen away!'

The ogre woke with a roar; he pulled on his seven-leagued boots, and strode off in pursuit of the brothers.

Swifter than the wind the first brother might run, but the ogre in his seven-leagued boots went swifter yet. His boots made no sound, for the ogre was striding through the air; but the second brother, with his sharp ears, heard the breath of his coming.

What to do?

'Leave it to me,' said the fifth brother. And he stamped on the ground. And where his foot struck there rose a great iron tower. The brothers rushed into the tower with the princess, and barred the door.

The ogre came up to the tower. He roared, he banged, he kicked – but he couldn't shake that tower. Then he began to howl, 'I want my little princess! I want my little princess! Just make a little window, just let her put her little head out, just let me give her one little kiss, and I'll be good and go home and leave you in peace!'

But the brothers didn't trust him, not they! And they didn't make a little window.

Then the ogre began to howl again; he was actually shedding tears, they were rolling down his cheeks and making a big pool on the ground. 'I want to say goodbye to my little princess! Just let me kiss her little finger, and I will let you go! But if I *can't* kiss her little finger, I will stay here till doomsday, and you will starve to death, and my little princess will starve to death also!'

Well, the brothers talked it over, and they thought there would be no harm in letting the princess put her finger out. So they made a slit in the tower, and the princess put her finger through the slit.

What happened? The ogre drew in his breath; he drew the princess out through the slit, took her in his arms, and ran off with her.

There he was now, going over the ground so fast in his seven-leagued boots that in one moment he was but a speck in the distance. But the sixth brother took his crossbow, and shot his arrow – his arrow that could shoot and kill whatever the eye saw, whether near or far. That arrow, flew, flew; it pierced the ogre through the heart and he fell dead. Then the first brother gathered the other brothers in his arms; he ran out of the iron tower; he ran, ran, swifter than the wind blows, to the place where the ogre lay dead. Oh alas, alas! What did they see? The arrow that had pierced the ogre had pierced the princess also. There she lay, pale and dead, in the ogre's arms.

But the seventh brother drew the arrow from her heart; he carried her a space away from the dead ogre; he laid her on the soft grass; he stooped over her, and with his guitar he played a life-restoring melody. The princess opened her eyes, she smiled, she rose to her feet. 'Have I been asleep?' she said.

'Yes, you have slept, but now you wake again,' said the eldest brother, and he took her in his arms. Then he gathered his six brothers into his arms also, and swifter than any wind that blows he ran with them to the king's court.

'Our princess is alive! Our princess is unharmed! Our princess has come back to us!' All the people in the city were shouting and cheering. And the king and the queen were embracing their little daughter with the tears running down their cheeks.

'And you, my good lads,' said the king to the seven brothers, 'which of you has saved my little daughter, that you may take her to wife and become my heir?'

'We have all saved her, your majesty,' said the eldest brother. 'Not one of us could have rescued her without the help of the other six.'

Here was a quandary! As the king said, no princess could have *seven* husbands.

'Then let the princess choose,' said the eldest brother. 'And we will abide by her choice.'

The princess looked from one brother to the other. Such fine, upstanding, handsome youths, she felt she could love them all. She looked and looked, and then smiled. 'I will choose the youngest,' she said, 'because he is nearest to my own age, and I like his curly hair.'

So the princess married the youngest brother; and if the other six brothers were a little disappointed, they were really too fond of each other to be jealous. The king made them all dukes; and he gave their father cartloads of gold – enough to keep him in comfort all his life.

4. The Gold Knob

There was a troll called Kidmus, and he lived in a mound. And near the mound was a tiny, tiny cottage. And in the cottage lived an old man and his old wife. The old man went fishing and hunting, the old woman sat and spun; so they had food and they had clothes; and they had just one treasure, and that was a gold knob on the old woman's spindle.

So one day the old woman was sitting in the sun outside her tiny, tiny cottage, spinning and singing a cracked little song. And as she sat and span, the gold knob, their one and only treasure, fell off the spindle and rolled away.

Lawk-a-mercy! The old woman looked here, she looked there, she looked everywhere – no, she couldn't find that gold knob.

By and by home comes the old man with some fish on a string. 'Old woman, what are you doing, poking about in the grass like that?'

'Old man, I sat and span, and I sang me a song, and the gold knob gave a jump and fell off the spindle. It rolled away and I can't find it anywhere.'

'Well then, old woman, troll Kidmus must have taken it.'

And the old man goes and knocks with his stick against the side of the troll's mound: *kerflick, kerflack! kerflick, kerflack!*

'Who knocks so loud on the side of my house?' shouts troll Kidmus.

'It is the old peasant, dear Kidmus. My old woman wants something for her gold knob.'

'What gold knob?'

'The gold knob you stole from her, dear Kidmus.'

'Well, what does she want for it?'

'A cow, dear Kidmus, a cow to give four barrels full of milk.'

'Right! Here she is!'

Then the side of the mound opened, and out walked a cow.

The old man walked off with the cow. He hobbled her with a long rope on the grass outside the tiny, tiny cottage. Next morning he milked her. He milked and milked, and still the milk came flowing. The milk filled one pail, it filled another pail; the old man shouted to the old woman, and she came running with saucepans and kettles and tubs and basins. The milk filled the saucepans, it filled the kettles, it filled the tubs and the basins. The milk didn't stop flowing till every vessel was full.

Well now, what to do with all that milk?

'We must make porridge,' says the old woman.

'We haven't any oatmeal,' says the old man.

'Then go and ask troll Kidmus for some,' says the old woman.

So off with the old man to the troll's mound again, and knocking with his stick on the side of the mound: *kerflick, kerflack! kerflick, kerflack!*

'Who knocks so loud on the side of my house?' shouts troll Kidmus.

'It is the old peasant, dear Kidmus. My old woman wants something more for her gold knob.'

'What does she want this time?'

'Some oatmeal to make porridge, dear Kidmus.'

'Right! Here it is!'

Then the side of the mound opened, and out rolled a barrel full of oatmeal. The old man rolled the barrel back to the tiny, tiny cottage. He opened the barrel and the old woman cooked porridge. She cooked porridge and she cooked porridge, and she cooked porridge. They ate and they ate, but they couldn't eat it all.

'Old woman,' says the old man, 'if we eat for a month we can never swallow down all this porridge. So what to do with it?'

'Give it away, old man.'

To whom shall we give it, old woman?'

'Why, to St Peter, of course.'

'But how to reach him, old woman?'

'Old man,' says the old woman, 'troll Kidmus still owes us something for my gold knob. Go and ask him for a ladder to reach to heaven.'

The old man went to the troll's mound and knocked with his stick: *kerflick, kerflack! kerflick, kerflack! kerflick, kerflack!*

'Who knocks so long and loud on the side of my house?'

'It is the old peasant, dear Kidmus. My old woman must have something else for her gold knob.'

'Old peasant, isn't that gold knob paid for twice over?'

'No, dear Kidmus, it isn't.'

'Yes, old peasant, it is.'

'I think it isn't, dear Kidmus.'

'I think it is, old man.'

'Dear Kidmus, I beg you earnestly to give us a long ladder. We want that long ladder to take some porridge to St Peter in heaven.'

'Oh well, oh well, oh well – take it.'

Then the side of the mound flew open, and out shot a long ladder.

The old man set the ladder up against the mound. He shouted to the old woman, and she came running with an earthen pot full of porridge.

'It's heavy, old man, you carry it!'

'No, old woman, it was your notion, you must carry it.'

'Well then, old man, we'll carry it turn and turn about.'

So they began to climb the ladder: the old man in front, the old woman behind him. She carried the porridge pot for a yard or two. Then she handed it to the old man, and he carried it for a yard or two. And up they went, and up they went, and up and up and up.

'Old man, it's a long way to heaven.'

'What else did you expect, old woman?'

'And it'll be a long way down to earth again, old man.'

'That's true, old woman.'

'Old man, I think the ladder's swaying!'

'I think so too, old woman.'

'Old man, old man, my head's spinning round! Here, it's your turn to carry the porridge pot.'

The old man took one hand off the ladder and reached back for the pot. The old woman caught hold of his ankles.

'Let go of my ankles, old woman!'

'I can't, old man, my head's spinning round worse than ever!'

'Bother your head!' The old man gave a kick, the ladder gave a jerk, the old woman gave a scream – down they toppled, old man, old woman, ladder, and pot, and the pot broke in pieces and covered them with porridge.

Oh, oh, oh! There they are, battered and bruised and all messed up with porridge, lying on the grass outside the troll's mound.

'Help me up, old man, help me up!'

The old man staggers to his feet, and pulls the old woman on to *her* feet. They stumble away into their tiny, tiny cottage. The old woman is wailing, the old man is rubbing his back.

'I will never go again to the troll's mound,' says he. 'I will never ask troll Kidmus to give me anything else for your wretched knob '

And, inside the mound, troll Kidmus is laughing! *Ha! ha! ha! Ha! ha! ha!*

5. The Children on the Pillar

Far away, in a big country, there lived a king and a queen who had two children, a boy and a girl, called Ivan and Olya. And in that kingdom there was a huge and terrible man-eating ogre, who every day was coming nearer and nearer to the king's city, killing everything as he came, trampling down farmlands and orchards, and leaving nothing but bare earth and scattered bones behind him.

So the people came to the king and said, 'Oh king, to stay here is death! Let us leave this city and go far away to the other end of the kingdom, where perhaps the ogre will not follow us.'

The king agreed; but he did not wish to risk taking his two children on so long a journey, which perhaps – should the ogre follow them – might only end in death. So what did he do? He built an ivory pillar, very high, very strong, with a very narrow door, and a narrow spiral staircase, and only one room at the very top. And into this pillar he put Ivan and Olya, with provisions to last them for five years. Then the king, the queen, the courtiers, and all the people from the city and the surrounding country set off on their weary journey.

Now it wasn't long after this before the ogre came trampling into the city, and finding it empty he flew into a terrible rage, and flung down all the houses in the streets. Then he strode on to the king's palace; and if he had been in a rage before, it was nothing to

44

the rage he was in now, for there was not a single soul in the palace for him to eat, and not a scrap of any kind of food, either. There was nothing in the palace at all, except a birch broom behind the kitchen door, so he seized the broom and went thrashing about with it, hitting at the walls and doors.

'What's the use of all this?' says the birch broom. 'Hitting about like that won't get you anywhere, and you're hurting me!'

'I want food, *I want food*, *I WANT FOOD!*' howled the ogre.

'I can tell you where to get food,' says the birch broom. 'See that ivory pillar in the field yonder? At the top of that pillar are the two royal children, Ivan and Olya, plump little children, tender little children. . . .'

The ogre didn't stop to hear any more. He rushed off to the pillar. He tried to get in at the door, but he couldn't more than get his big toe through it, so he grabbed the pillar with his two huge hands and heaved and tugged; he made that tower rock like a ship in a gale, but he couldn't pull it down.

Prince Ivan looked out of the window at the top of the pillar. 'Go away!' he shouted. 'You're making us feel seasick – what do you want?'

'Food, *food*, *FOOD!*' yelled the ogre.

'Well then, here's food,' called Ivan, and he and Olya gathered up all the food they could lay hands on, and flung it out of the window.

The ogre gobbled up everything. Now he was full, so he lay down and slept.

'We must get away!' said Prince Ivan; and he and Olya ran down the spiral staircase, and out of the door at the bottom of the pillar. They ran, ran, ran, and over their heads a bright falcon came flying.

'Bright falcon!' cried Ivan. 'Take us between your wings and carry us away, before the ogre wakes and catches us!'

The bright falcon swooped down, took the children between his wings, and flew off.

The ogre woke up. He saw the pillar door open wide, he sniffed and snuffed. He smelled the way the children had gone, he saw the bright falcon carrying them away. He leaped over the ground with enormous strides till he came up with the bright falcon. But the bright falcon rose high into the air, the ogre couldn't reach him. So the ogre banged his head on the ground, and the ground burst into flames. The flames rose high, higher; they singed the bright falcon's wings, and he let the children fall.

The ogre picked up the children and carried them back to the ivory pillar. 'Now I will eat you both!' he roared.

But Ivan said, 'No, don't eat us yet. We have lots more food in the room at the top of the pillar – piles of meat, juicy and tender, and heaps of cakes, sweet and rich. But you know you can't reach them. If you eat us now, you will never be able to taste those cakes.'

The talk of sweet cakes made the ogre's mouth water, and he roared out, 'Fetch the meat, fetch the cakes! I will eat them first, and I will eat you afterwards.'

The children ran into the pillar. They ran up the spiral staircase to their room at the top. They threw down the meat and the sweet cakes through the window – piles of meat, piles of cake. The ogre gobbled up everything; and being full, he lay down and slept.

'This time we *will* get away!' said prince Ivan. And he and Olya ran down the spiral staircase again, and out through the door at the bottom of the pillar. They ran, ran, ran, they came to a great river. And on the river bank stood a wolf.

'Why are you running so fast?' said the wolf.

'We are running from the ogre,' said prince Ivan. 'And – oh me! – he is coming!'

Yes, the ogre had woken up, and there he was, racing with mighty strides across the desolate country.

'Jump on my back,' said the wolf.

Ivan and Olya jumped on to the wolf's back, and he swam with them across the river.

The ogre came to the river bank. But he couldn't swim, and the river was too deep for even an ogre to wade through. So there he was, standing on the bank, roaring with rage, and bellowing, 'I'll have you yet!' And he went back to the ivory pillar, and gripped hold of it, and shook and heaved and kicked and butted, till in the strength of his rage he pulled it down, and all the food that was stored in the top of it came tumbling down about his ears. So he kept filling himself full, and lying down to sleep, and waking and filling himself full again, and sleeping again, and was no more trouble to anyone for a while.

Now on the other side of the deep river there was a little tumble-down cottage on the edge of a wood. The children and the wolf went into the cottage and lived there. Ivan found a bow and arrows in the cottage and went hunting in the wood. Olya found a fishing line in the cottage and went fishing in the river. The wolf went hunting for his own food; and by and by a fox came to join them, and after the fox came a bear. The fox went foraging and brought in chickens and hens' eggs; the bear went foraging and brought in honeycombs and berries and crab apples; oh yes, they did well enough, and they never quarrelled. If you'd searched the world over you couldn't have found a happier company than those five.

But one day the fox said, 'Friends, this is all very well; but the ogre still lives, and the food he has got from the ivory pillar won't last him for ever. And I think that by and by he will find a way of getting across the river. So now I am going to dig in the earth and make a hide-out, with a very small entrance, only just big enough for Ivan and Olya to squeeze through. Then if the ogre *does* come, he won't be able to catch them. And as to us, brothers – we can take to our heels. The ogre won't bother about *us*!'

So the fox set to work and made a splendid hide-out, with a very small entrance, and a long tunnel going down into the earth, and a little room at the end of the tunnel. They put dry grass in the room to make a bed, and carried in food and water. And the wolf and the bear praised the fox – they thought him a wonderfully clever fellow.

'Now let the ogre do his worse!' said they. 'He won't catch our Ivan, and he won't catch our Olya!'

The fox was right about one thing: by this time the ogre had gobbled up all the food from the ivory pillar; and he was searching round for something more to eat when he caught a witch. And in return for her life, the witch gave him two gifts: the first gift was a little red magic pebble which, when he put in the mouth, would change a person into any shape he wished. The second gift was a little sharp magic bone that had the power of jumping into anybody's head and killing them. And on the strength of these two gifts, the ogre planned a deep and deadly revenge.

One day Ivan and the three animals went foraging in the wood, and left Olya to get dinner ready for them by the time they came back. And Olya took a pitcher and went to the river to dip up water. She looked across the river – what did she see? The handsomest lad ever you set eyes on, standing on the opposite bank, and waving to her.

'Oh lovely maiden,' cried the handsome lad. 'I am a prince. I have dreamed of you night after night, and I have wandered over half the world seeking you. Now I find you – and alas, alas, I cannot reach you! But at least throw me your scarf as a keepsake – and I will wear it next to my heart!'

So Olya (flattered, you're sure!) took off the scarf she was wearing round her neck, and leaned out over the water, and gave the scarf a toss. The wind took it, the handsome lad caught it – and what happened? The scarf turned itself into a bridge, and the lad ran lightly across the river. Oh horror – it was no handsome lad that stood there, but the ogre himself!

'Now I have you!' bawled the ogre. But Olya turned and fled. She ran to the fox's hide-out, and squeezed through the narrow entrance. The ogre rushed after her, but try as he would, he couldn't get more than three of his great fingers through that narrow entrance. And as to reaching Olya in the little room at the end of the long tunnel – no, that was impossible. 'Ah!' bawled he, 'If I can't have you, princess Olya, I'll have prince Ivan!' And he sniffed and snuffed, sniffed and snuffed. 'I smell him! I smell him!' he growled, and stalked off towards the wood.

There now out of the wood came Ivan and the three animals: Ivan with his bow across his shoulder, his quiver of arrows at his belt, and a brace of turkeys in either hand, the fox with a couple of rabbits he had caught, the wolf with a deer slung over his back, the bear carrying four honeycombs – all looking forward to a sumptuous dinner. Oh mercy – what do they see? The great hideous angry ogre striding towards them. The wolf, the bear and the fox fling down their spoils and take to their heels; Ivan tosses the turkeys to the ogre and makes a dash for the hide-out. But the ogre stretches out his long arm and catches up Ivan in his great fist.

'You don't escape me again, prince Ivan,' roars the ogre. 'But, ah, what a skinny little wretch you are! Scarce worth eating! Here's better fare that you and your friends have brought me! So you can rest quiet for a bit whilst I eat my fill!' And he shakes the little sharp magic bone out of his sleeve, and the bone gives a jump into Ivan's head.

What happens? Alas, alas! Ivan falls dead.

'Ha! ha!' roared the ogre. And he gathered up the turkeys and the rabbits and the deer and the honeycombs, and stuffed them all into his mouth and swallowed them.

'Full now,' he grunted. 'Shan't eat Ivan yet.' He gave a huge yawn, stretched himself out beside Ivan, and fell asleep. And his snores shook the ground.

Then the fox and the bear and the wolf came creeping cautiously back. Ah, how bitterly they wept when they saw the dead Ivan!

'Oh my dear, dear little friend!' sobbed the wolf, and bowed his head to kiss Ivan's cheek. What happened then? The bone gave a jump out of Ivan's head, and went into the wolf's head. The wolf fell dead, and Ivan sprang up alive.

'No, no, brother wolf!' cried the bear. 'It was you who carried Ivan across the deep river! You were his first friend! It is not you, but I who must die for him!' And the bear laid his head against the wolf's head. What happened? The bone gave a jump out of the wolf's head, and went into the bear's head. The bear fell dead, and the wolf sprang up alive.

Then the fox said to himself, 'Are my wits so rusty that I cannot use them now?' And he laid his head against the bear's head. What happened? The bone gave a jump out of the bear's head, and the bear sprang up alive. But before the bone could touch the fox, the fox moved his head aside. What happened? The bone sped on and went into the snoring ogre's head

So that was the last snore ever that ogre snored. There he was now – a great dead lump. And no one laid a head against his to bring him to life again – of that you may be sure!

How they cheered, how they danced! Olya came creeping out of the fox's shelter and danced and cheered with them. Then they all set out to seek the king and queen, the children's parents, and bring them the good news. A long, long, journey they had of it, across a desolate country that had all been laid waste by the ogre; but their journey ended at last. They found the king and queen, and all the people that were left in the realm, living in tents on the very outskirts of the king's country: living in deadly fear, too, that any day the ogre might seek them out and destroy them. But now all was rejoicing. King, queen, courtiers, townsfolk and country folk – a great multitude – travelled back with Ivan, Olya, the wolf, the bear and the fox to their old homes. They rebuilt the ravaged city, and restored the palace, making everything more splendid than it had been before. The townsfolk took up their old trades, the farmers returned to their deserted farms, and reploughed their ravaged lands. Everyone from now on lived without fear and in great content.

And as to the wolf, the bear and the fox, they were given rooms in the palace, and held in high honour all their lives.

6. Sigurd the King's Son

Once upon a time there lived a happy king and queen who had one little son, called Sigurd. But alas, when Sigurd was still a little boy, the queen died. The king mourned, mourned; and his people came to him and said, 'Sire, for our sakes, for your little son's sake, it is your duty to take another wife.'

The king sighed. 'If it is my duty, I will take another wife.' But of all the noble ladies, the princesses and the duchesses, that his people brought to the king's notice – no, not one pleased him.

And he took to wandering about in the woods by himself, mourning for his dead queen.

Now one hot day, when he was wandering in the woods, he felt weary, and sat down under a tree to rest. And as he so rested, he saw, walking down a glade towards him, a lady, so beautiful, so beautiful, that in all the world none could be more lovely. And the king thought, 'If I must marry, then that lady, and none other, shall be my wife.' And he rose up and went to meet her, and told her of his sorrow, and of his little son, Sigurd, and of his duty to his people. And he asked her her name, and where she lived, and if she would be his queen.

And the beautiful lady answered, 'My name is Ingeborg, sire, and I live here in the wood. But alas, I cannot be your queen, for I am a troll's daughter.'

But the king said, 'What does that matter? One so beautiful must needs be good.'

'Yes, I hope I am good,' said Ingeborg, 'but that is all the more reason why I cannot marry you. For my people are not good, and I would not bring danger to you and your child.'

'Then you will leave me to die of grief!' cried the king.

Well, for a long time Ingeborg refused. But in the end, because of the king's grief, and his pleadings, she consented. And the king brought her back to the palace and married her.

His people rejoiced: they all loved Ingeborg, but none loved her better than the little prince Sigurd. He followed her everywhere, and would never leave her side.

Now one day the king was going out to hunt, and Queen Ingeborg said, 'Sigurd, your pony waits in the courtyard – off with you, and hunt with the king.'

But no, Sigurd wouldn't go. He said he must stay with Ingeborg.

'Very well then,' said Ingeborg. 'Get under the sofa. Keep still as a mouse, and don't you come out until I call.'

So Sigurd crept under the sofa and kept still.

Then there came a mighty rumbling: the floor heaved, the door flew open, and in strode a huge troll wife, wading up to her ankles through the floor.

'Be greeted, sister Ingeborg,' said the troll wife. 'Is the king's son, Sigurd, at home?'

'No,' said Ingeborg, 'Sigurd is in the forest, hunting with the king.'

Then Ingeborg set food and drink before the troll wife, and the troll wife gobbled up everything and smacked her lips. And when there wasn't a crumb of food left, the troll wife said, 'I thank you, sister Ingeborg, for the best titbits, the best lamb, the best pot of ·

beer, and the best drink. . . . Is the king's son, Sigurd, at home?'

'I told you,' said Ingeborg, 'Sigurd has gone hunting with the king.'

So the troll wife got up. The room heaved, the floor shook, and the troll wife waded out, *stamp, stamp*, with her ankles going through the floor at every step.

'You can come out from under the sofa now, Sigurd,' said Ingeborg. 'But tell no one of what you have seen.'

Sigurd came out. He stood up very straight. 'I will tell no one,' he said.

The next day the king again went hunting; and again Ingeborg urged Sigurd to go with him, and again Sigurd refused. He was going to stay with Ingeborg, he said. So Ingeborg hid him under the table, and bade him keep quiet for his life, and neither speak nor move until she called him.

And scarcely was Sigurd under the table before there came again a mighty rumbling: the floor heaved, the door flew open, and in strode the troll wife, wading up to her knees through the floor.

'Be greeted, sister Ingeborg,' says she. 'Is the king's son, Sigurd, at home?'

'No,' said Ingeborg. 'Sigurd has gone hunting with the king, his father.'

Then Ingeborg set food and drink before the troll wife, and the troll wife gobbled up everything, and smacked her lips, and said, 'I thank you, sister Ingeborg, for the best titbits, the best lamb, the best pot of beer, and the best drink. . . . Is the king's son, Sigurd, at home?'

'No,' said Ingeborg, 'Sigurd is in the forest, hunting with the king.'

So then the troll wife got up. The room heaved, the floor shook, and the troll wife waded out, *stamp, stamp*, with her knees going through the floor at every step.

Sigurd came out from under the table. Ingeborg scolded him, '*Now* you see what comes of your love for me! You are in great danger. Tomorrow, when the king goes hunting, you must and shall go with him.'

But Sigurd stood up very straight and said, 'I love you better than all else in the world. Why should I not stay with you? I am not afraid of danger.'

Next morning, when the king again went hunting, Ingeborg took Sigurd by the hand, led him out into the courtyard, and set him on his pony. 'Be off with you!' said she, and gave the pony a clap on the rump. So the pony, with Sigurd on his back, galloped off after the hunt.

Ingeborg went back into the palace; but she had scarce sat down when in marched Sigurd. He was laughing. 'You don't get rid of me so easily, dear mother,' he said.

So Ingeborg hid him in the cupboard, and scarcely had she shut the cupboard door, when there came a mighty rumbling: the floor heaved, the room door flew open, and in strode the troll wife, wading through the floor up to her waist.

'Good morning, sister Ingeborg,' said she. 'Is the king's son, Sigurd, at home?'

'No,' said Ingeborg. 'He has gone hunting with the king, his father.'

'That's a lie!' screamed the troll wife.

But Ingeborg set meat and drink before her, and the troll wife gobbled up everything, and smacked her lips. And when there was nothing left to eat or drink, she thanked Ingeborg in the same words as on the day before, and then said, 'Is the king's son, Sigurd, at home?'

'I told you,' said Ingeborg. 'Sigurd is out hunting with the king.'

'You tell me lies!' roared the troll wife in a voice like thunder· 'If he is near enough to hear my words, I lay a curse upon him! He shall become a cock, and he shall never get back his true shape until he finds me.'

Then she went away, wading through the floor up to her waist, *bump, stump*; *bump, stump*, making the whole palace shake and rumble with the noise of her going.

Ingeborg went to the cupboard. She was trembling. She opened the cupboard door – what came out? Alas! Alas! A little cock with a red comb.

'Oh my dear little stepson,' wept Ingeborg. 'What did I tell you?'

The little cock's eyes sparkled. He flung up his head, clapped his wings, and crowed, as much as to say, 'I defy the whole world!'

'There is no help for it,' said Ingeborg. 'Now you must go to my sister, or you will never get back your true shape.'

Then she opened a chest and took out a gold ring and a golden ball. 'Roll this ball before you,' she said, 'and it will lead you to my sister. Give her this ring, for that will please her, and maybe she will have pity on you. Goodbye, my little stepson, and may God in his mercy shield you from danger! But one thing I must ask of you. If ever in your wanderings my little dog should come to you with the tears streaming down his face, come home quickly, for I shall be in mortal peril. Go now, before the king returns!'

So the little cock took the ring in his beak and rolled the ball before him, and went, went, went, up hill, down dale, wherever the ball led him. And in the evening he came to a great cliff.

At the top of the cliff stood the troll wife, looking down.

'Magnificent!' she shouted in her huge voice, that made the cliff echo and the ground tremble. 'Sigurd, the king's son, has come, and tonight he shall go into my pot!'

She let down a boat hook on a long line: the hook caught the little cock round the neck, and the troll wife pulled him up to stand on the cliff beside her. Then she gave him a smack, and he changed back into his true shape.

'Good evening, step-aunt,' says he, bold as brass. 'My step-mother sent you this gold ring, and begs your acceptance of it.' And he bowed low and held the ring out to her.

'Well, you've pretty manners, I will say,' she grunted, taking the ring.

The ring wouldn't go on to any of her great fingers. But she blew on it, and made it bigger, and then she put it on the thumb of her right hand. 'Very pretty indeed!' said she. 'Perhaps I won't eat you tonight after all. Tomorrow'll be time enough for that.'

And she took him down into her cave inside the cliff.

Well, she didn't eat Sigurd the next day, either. In fact she grew fond of him, and admired the bold way in which he stood up to her when she tried to frighten him. She kept him with her for seven days, which were really seven years, for a troll's day is a year long. And he grew into a fine strong handsome lad. 'Now we will wrestle,' said she. 'And if you can throw me, I will let you go.'

So they wrestled, and she flung him to the floor.

'Bah!' said she, 'You are a weakling after all.'

'I am not a weakling, I am *not*!' shouted Sigurd.

Then the troll wife fetched a phial full of strength-giving wine, and made Sigurd drink from it. 'Now we will wrestle again,' said she.

And they wrestled, and Sigurd held his own until his head reeled and his breath came in gasps. But the troll wife had him down in the end.

'Drink again,' said she.

So Sigurd drank again, and they wrestled again. They wrestled long, long; but Sigurd held his ground, for the strength of the wine flowed through him, and at last he beat the troll wife to her knees.

'Ah ha!' said she. 'Now I've made a man of you! A better man than ever sister Ingeborg could make. Do you want to stay with me, or do you want to go?'

'I want to go,' said Sigurd.

The troll wife laughed so loud that Sigurd thought the cave roof would surely fall in on them. And when she'd done laughing, she took him out to the top of the cliff and said, 'You won't go back to sister Ingeborg – that way's barred. You'll follow your nose, my lad, and you'll come to a lake, and by the lake you'll see a little girl playing with a canoe. There's something for you to do there – I shan't tell you what it is. But it may be dangerous, so here's a gift for you.' And she gave him a little stick and a small flat stone. One side of the stone was black, and the other side was white.

'If you strike with the stick on the black side of the stone, you make darkness,' said she. 'If you strike on the white side, you make hail. Now be off – and don't forget the old fool troll wife, who came to like you against her will.'

And she gave him a push that knocked him off his feet, and sent him hurtling down the cliff.

He fell on a big clump of grass and wasn't even bruised. So he picked himself up and looked about him. There seemed but one path for him to follow and he followed it, and came by and by to a lake, where a little girl was sitting in a canoe by the bank, dabbling her feet in the water.

'Who are you?' said the little girl.

'I'm Sigurd, the king's son,' said he. 'Who are you?'

'I'm Princess Helga,' said she. 'This isn't my home, and I don't like it here. But an old troll stole me away. I have to call him "Father", and he's a terror. Can you row?'

'I don't know,' says Sigurd; 'I've never tried.'

'Well, come and try then,' says Helga.

So they played together all through the day. But at sunset Helga said, 'Goodbye, I have to go home now.'

'I'm coming with you,' said Sigurd.

'Oh no,' said Helga. 'Strangers aren't allowed in Father Troll's castle. If they come in, he eats them.'

'Then I'll come with you as far as the castle gate,' says Sigurd.

'So do,' says Helga. And they walked off together.

But when they came to the castle gate Helga said, 'I like you. I don't want to lose you.' And she gave him a tap with a little ring she wore, and turned him into a bundle of wool. 'Father Troll gave me this ring,' she said. 'He thought it would make me like him, but it doesn't.'

The bundle of wool didn't answer. It couldn't speak. It felt very queer. Helga picked it up, carried it into the castle, and laid it on her bed.

By and by in stamped the troll. Ugly wasn't the word for him. *Sniff! Snuff! Sniff! Snuff!* 'I can smell human flesh here.'

'You smell me,' said Helga.

'No, *not* you!' roared the troll. 'Other flesh!' and he went sniffing, here, snuffing there, following his nose. And his nose led him to Helga's bed.

'What's this on your bed?' says he.

'Some wool,' says Helga.

'Where did you get it?' he roared.

'I picked it up,' says Helga.

'Well then, that's what it is,' said the troll. 'A human being must have dropped it. I can't eat wool, more's the pity, so you can keep it.'

All night the bundle of wool lay on Helga's bed; and in the morning Helga carried that bundle of wool down to the lake. She gave the wool a tap with her ring, and it changed back into Sigurd. And she and Sigurd played together. 'You needn't be a bundle of wool again till evening,' she said.

But that evening, when Helga carried the bundle of wool into the castle, the troll said, 'I won't have that human smell in here – it makes my mouth water.'

'But I want to spin the wool and make a dress,' said Helga.

'Well, you can't,' roared the troll. And he took up the wool and flung it into the courtyard.

The bundle of wool lay in the courtyard all night, and it dreamed very strange dreams about flying through the air.

Early next morning Helga came into the courtyard, gave the wool a tap with her ring, and changed it back into Sigurd. 'We can stay and play in the castle today,' she said. 'Father Troll's gone to a troll meeting in the mountains – he won't be back till evening.'

'I dreamed I was flying,' said Sigurd.

'I dreamed better than that,' said Helga. 'I dreamed we found a flying carpet in a chest in the garret, and it carried us home.'

'Let's go and look,' said Sigurd.

So they went into the castle and upstairs and upstairs till they came to a great cobwebby garret under the roof. The garret window was wide open, and under the window was an iron chest.

'That's it!' cried Helga. 'That's my dream!'

But the chest was locked – and where was the key?

They searched here, they searched there; they saw the key at last, hanging on a peg among the cobwebs under the ceiling. But reach that key they couldn't. Sigurd jumped and tried. Helga got on Sigurd's shoulders and stretched up and tried. No good. They got cross and dirty and covered with cobwebs. 'I won't be beaten!' cried Sigurd. And he dragged the chest across the floor till it stood under the place where the key hung. He got on the chest, took Helga on his shoulders and said, 'Now try!'

Helga reached, reached, reached, she stood on tiptoe and nearly fell off Sigurd's shoulders, but she gave a jump and got hold of the key at last, and then they both toppled to the floor.

What matter a few bruises? They had the key and they unlocked the chest. Inside was a dusty old carpet, all rolled up. The carpet had gold letters on it. Sigurd began to read the letters – and the carpet, all rolled up as it was, began to rise out of the chest.

Then he stopped reading, and the carpet sank down on to the floor.

Oh ho! They unrolled the carpet and both sat on it. Sigurd read all the words that were written round its edge: 'TELL ME WHERE YOU WANT TO GO.'

'To Helga's home!' shouted Sigurd. And the carpet rose with them into the air, and sailed out through the open window.

Away and away and away! The sun bright overhead; fields and forests, mountains, valleys and streams gliding backwards beneath them. Helga sang, Sigurd laughed. But – oh dear me! suddenly there came a howling and a roaring behind them. They looked back – what did they see? The troll in his seven-leagued boots hurtling through the air and gaining on them.

What to do? Sigurd remembered the troll wife's gift. He took the flat stone and the little stick out of his pocket. He struck the stone with the stick on the black side, and night fell round them: night so black that they could see nothing in front of them, and nothing behind them except the troll's blazing eyes. But those blazing eyes could see in the dark, the troll came tearing on, and the blazing eyes came nearer, and nearer, and nearer.

'Now Father Troll will kill us both!' wailed Helga.

But Sigurd struck the stone with the stick again. He struck it on the white side. And as he struck he turned round and flung stick and stone into the troll's eyes. Now in front of them the sun shone out again, but behind them fell a storm of hailstones big as boulders. The huge hailstones beat the troll down to earth and killed him. And the flying carpet sped on, and brought Helga and Sigurd to the palace of the king and queen who were Helga's parents.

See now the happiness of king and queen and Helga, and of all the people in that kingdom, whose little princess had come back to them! See Sigurd's happiness too, proud to be treated as a hero. 'He is a prince as handsome as he is brave,' the people said, 'and when he is grown up he shall marry our princess.'

Yes, Sigurd was like to be spoiled among them.

But one morning, as he was getting out of bed, something came scratching at Sigurd's door. He opened the door – what did he see? A little white dog, looking up at him with tears streaming out of its brown eyes, and trickling down its cheeks. Queen Ingeborg's little dog! And Sigurd remembered Queen Ingeborg's words: 'If ever in your wanderings my little dog should come to you with the tears streaming down his face, come home quickly, for I shall be in deadly peril.'

Sigurd took the little dog under one arm, and the flying carpet under the other arm, and ran to the room where Helga was sleeping.

'I'm going home, Helga!' he shouted. And not even waiting for her to answer, he rushed out into the palace yard, sat himself and the little dog on the carpet, and cried out, 'Take me home, home to Queen Ingeborg!'

The carpet rose into the air. Swifter than the swiftest wind that blows, it flew over hills and dales, rivers, forests and mountains, and never paused in its flight until it came to earth in the great square outside the palace of the king, who was Sigurd's father.

What did Sigurd see as he and the little dog jumped off the carpet? He saw a great crowd gathered, and in the middle of the square he saw a stake with wood and straw piled round it; tied to the stake he saw Queen Ingeborg; he saw his father, the king, standing by the stake with his hands before his face, and he saw soldiers with lighted torches about to set fire to the pile.

Sigurd ran, he struck out right and left, he sent the soldiers sprawling, he leaped on to the pile and clasped Ingeborg in his arms. 'I am Sigurd, the king's son!' he shouted, 'What man among you dares to harm the good Queen Ingeborg?'

The king took his hands from before his face and stared. A great sigh went up from the people, and then a mighty shout: 'Sigurd the king's son! Sigurd the king's son! He is not dead! Sigurd the king's son lives!'

Yes, it was all a mistake. Since Sigurd had disappeared, none knew where, the people had declared that Queen Ingeborg had killed him. After all, they said, what else could you expect of a woman who came from the trolls? Beautiful she might be, and good she might seem, but that was all deception. Yes, yes, yes, they said, she had killed and eaten Sigurd, after the manner of trolls. And so they had compelled the sadly grieving king to have her burned at the stake. But now Sigurd told his story, and all was rejoicing. With pealing of bells, with feasting and dancing, the people welcomed Sigurd the king's son home again. The good Queen Ingeborg was enthroned once more, and she and the king and Sigurd lived happily together.

And when Sigurd was quite grown up, he set off on the flying carpet, and brought the princess Helga home with him to be his wife.

7. The Girl in the Basket

There was a man who had a pear tree; and every year, when the pears were ripe, he must take four basketfuls of those pears to the king, because this was the rent he paid for his cottage. But there came one year when he picked all his pears, and put them in baskets, and they didn't fill but three of those baskets, and a half of the fourth one. What to do? The man goes and fetches the smallest of his daughters, puts her in the half-filled basket on top of the pears, and covers her up with leaves. Then he lifts the four baskets into his little handcart, and off with him, wheeling his little handcart, to the palace.

'Take your baskets to the king's pantry and empty out the pears,' says the king's cook.

The man does that and goes home. And the little girl, whose name is Margaretina, stays hidden among the pears.

So by and by Margaretina gets hungry and she begins to eat the pears. She eats one, she eats two; and as the days go by, she's eaten more than a lot. And the king's cook says, 'My word, how those pears are vanishing! There must be some animal in the pantry gobbling them up.' And he goes to search among the pears. What does he find? He finds Margaretina.

The cook scolds, Margaretina weeps. She is very small, very

66

pretty. So the cook says, 'No, don't cry; you can come and work for me in the kitchen.'

So Margaretina worked for the cook in the kitchen. And her father heard of it and said to himself, 'Margaretina's got a good job, I needn't worry about her any more.' And he didn't worry.

Well, Margaretina worked in the king's kitchen for one year, she worked for two years, she worked for many years. She grew into the most beautiful maiden. And she did her work so well, and was so kind and sweet, that everybody about the court came to love her, even the young prince, the king's son and heir. But there were servants who were jealous, and these servants said, 'Who is Margaretina to find favour above us all? We must get rid of her!'

So they went to the King and said, 'Margaretina has been boasting that she can do all the palace laundry, wash, dry, iron and fold it away, all in one morning.'

The king sent for Margaretina. He said, 'I hear that you can do all the palace laundry, wash, iron, dry and fold it away, all in one morning.'

'Oh no, nobody could do that!' said Margaretina.

The king said, 'Then why did you say you could?'

Margaretina said, 'I never said so!'

But the king said, 'Boasters must keep their word. Go and do what you have said, or I will have you whipped.'

Margaretina went away and wept bitterly. And the prince, the king's son and heir, found her weeping, and said, 'What is the matter, dear Margaretina, that you weep so bitterly?'

Margaretina told him, and the prince said. 'Wipe your eyes, I will help you. Ask the king to have all the dirty linen brought into the bath house.'

So Margaretina did that, and all the dirty linen was brought into the bath house, a mighty pile of it.

Then the prince came in. He took a wand from under his robe and waved the wand over the pile of soiled linen. In a moment – see, everything: towels, shirts, sheets, pillowcases, stockings, tablecloths – all the whole pile of them, washed, ironed, folded and ready to be put away.

And the prince said, 'Now go and tell the king. But don't say who helped you.'

So Margaretina ran off happily to tell the king that everything was done. And if she had found favour in the king's eyes before, she found more favour now. But the servants grumbled more than ever.

Now in a palace, some way from the king's court, and on the other side of a deep, slimy river, there lived a horrible ogress; and the ogress possessed a great treasure which she had stolen from the king. The treasure was a box of musical instruments that played by themselves. But nobody dared to get back that treasure, because the ogress ate everyone who came near her palace. So the king's servants said to one another, 'Here's our chance to get rid of Margaretina!' And they went to the king and said, 'Margaretina has been boasting that she is not afraid of the ogress. She says she could any day get your musical instruments back for you, if she'd a mind to. But she won't do it, not she!'

Then the king sent for Margaretina and said, 'I hear you have been boasting that you can get back my box of musical instruments. Well, go and do it.'

No good for poor Margaretina to protest that she had never said any such thing. The king was firm: Margaretina *had* said it, and Margaretina must go and do it. So Margaretina went up to her room and wept. And the prince heard her weeping and came in, and said, 'Margaretina, dear Margaretina, why do you weep?'

Margaretina told him, and the prince said, 'Dry your eyes. I will help you. Ask the king to give you three quarts of oil, three pounds of beef, three brooms, three soft brushes, and three oven cloths.' Then he told her what she must do with these things, and what else she must do. And Margaretina went to the king and said, 'Since I go to my death, give me three quarts of oil, three pounds of beef, three brooms, three soft brushes and three oven cloths.'

Well, the king gave her all she asked for, and Margaretina set out. She went, went, went, and came to the deep slimy river. And she stooped down and took a little of the slimy water in her hands (for so the prince had told her to do) and she said, 'Little river, lovely little river, if I were not in such haste I would strip myself naked and bathe in your crystal waters. But I have an errand to do, and I must hurry.'

The river, who had never before been called anything but ugly names, was flattered; and it drew back its waters on either side, and said, 'Cross over dry shod, beautiful little Margaretina!'

And Margaretina crossed over.

There now was the ogress's palace: the grandest palace ever you saw, with a great courtyard flanked by marble pillars. At the entrance to the courtyard was the ogress's huge oven, and kneeling by the oven were three women tearing out their long hair to clean the oven with, for they had neither cloths nor brushes. And all the time they were tearing out their hair, they were shrieking with pain.

But Margaretina went to them and said. 'Don't shriek, don't tear out your hair!' And she gave them the three brooms, and the three soft brushes, and the three oven cloths. And then, as they were cleaning the oven, they were singing.

69

Margaretina was going to cross the courtyard when out from behind the marble pillars leaped three huge dogs, barking and growling, and bristling up their backs like wolves. They thought to tear Margaretina to pieces; but she threw them the three pounds of beef, and they wagged their tails and let her pass.

So she crossed the courtyard and came to the great iron door of the palace; and that door was opening and shutting, opening and shutting so fast that no one could get through, and all the time its hinges were squealing, because they were rusted up. But Margaretina poured her three quarts of oil over the hinges; and the door swung wide open and stayed open. And Margaretina went through.

The ogress was upstairs in her bed. She was lazy, she didn't get up till noon. Margaretina went through one room, she went through another room, and she came into a third room, and on a table in this third room was the box of musical instruments that played by themselves – the king's treasure that the ogress had stolen.

Margaretina snatched up the box and ran off with it. But her feet on the marble floors went *slip-slap, slip-slap*, and the ogress heard (she wasn't asleep) and she came pounding downstairs in her nightgown. She saw Margaretina making for the palace door, and she cried out, 'Door, squeeze her! Door, squeeze her!'

But the door said, 'No, I won't squeeze her. For a hundred years my hinges have been rusting, and you never gave me a drop of oil. But Margaretina has given me three bottles full.'

And the door stood wide open to let Margaretina run through, but it slammed itself shut in the ogress's face.

The ogress gave the door a bang with her mighty fist and broke it down. She saw Margaretina running across the courtyard, and

she shouted to her three great dogs, 'Dogs, kill her! Dogs, kill her!'
But the dogs said, 'No, we won't kill her. For a hundred years you
have fed us on scraps of bread, but Margaretina has given us juicy
meat.' And they sprang at the ogress, biting and snarling.

The ogress beat off the dogs with her mighty fists; she saw
Margaretina passing the oven, and she shouted to the women who
cleaned it, 'Push her in the oven and burn her! Push her in the oven
and burn her!'

But the women answered, 'For a hundred years we have been
tearing out our hair to clean your oven for you, and you gave us
neither brush nor cloth, but Margaretina gave us these things. Why
should we push her into the oven? No, we won't do it!' And they
stuck their brushes out, and the ogress tripped over them, and went
head over heels. And that delayed her for a bit. But she picked
herself up and raced on after Margaretina.

By this time Margaretina had reached the slimy river, and the
ogress bawled out, 'Slimy, slimy river, drown Margaretina!'

But the river answered, 'Why should I drown her? She called me
pretty names. She said to me, "Little river, lovely little river,
crystal clear," and that is more than *you* have ever done!' And the
river drew back its waters on either side, and Margaretina ran over
dry shod to the opposite bank. But when the ogress thought to
follow her, the angry river rose up in a mighty wave, and beat the
ogress down, and – yes, it drowned her.

Margaretina sat on the bank to rest. Now she was safe! She had
the king's box safe too. Then she had a dreadful thought. Suppose
there was nothing in the box? It felt so light! Suppose the ogress
had taken everything out of it? Margaretina gave the box a little
shake. She put her ear to it, and listened. No, nothing stirred in
the box, nothing sounded. Oh me, if it should be empty after all!

Then the king would be so angry, so angry, he might surely kill her!

So Margaretina opened the box to see if all was well within it.

Heavens above! What was happening? Out of the box came flying fiddles and flutes, cymbals and trumpets, guitars and zithers, banjoes, lyres, harps and drums. They were all whirling this way and that way in the air round Margaretina, and all playing away like mad. Margaretina ran about, snatching at one, snatching at another, putting them back in the box; but no sooner had she got one instrument back into the box and turned to catch another, than the first one was out of the box again; and the air rang with such a crazy hubbub of mixed music as she had never heard in all her life before.

'Oh, what shall I do?' wailed Margaretina. And at last, worn out, she put her fingers in her ears, and sat down, and cried.

And then, all at once, there was the prince, the king's son and heir, standing beside her. He waved his wand, the clamour stopped, and every instrument went back into the box. The prince shut down the lid, and then he said, 'Margaretina, lovely little Margaretina, I have saved your life. Now you must love me, and marry me.'

Margaretina said, 'Yes, I will love you and marry you.'

The prince said, 'Well then, if you love me, when the king tells you to choose a reward for fetching the box, ask him for the great coal chest in the palace cellar, and what is inside it.'

Margaretina thought this a very strange thing to ask for; because what could be inside the coal chest but coal? And what could Margaretina do with a heap of coal? But as the prince had told her to ask for the chest, ask for it she did. She brought the box of musical instruments to the delighted king, and when the king said, 'Choose your reward,' she said, 'I choose the great coal chest in the palace cellar, and what is inside it.'

The king laughed, and said, 'So be it!'

Then the coal chest was brought up; the lid was lifted. What was inside that chest? The prince, the king's son and heir.

The king laughed and laughed. And when he had done laughing he said, 'A king can't go back on his royal word. And I don't know that this king wants to; for in all the world one couldn't find a sweeter little maiden.'

So Margaretina and the prince were married. The king dismissed the jealous servants and got others in their place. And from that day to this, all has been peace and happiness in the royal palace.

8. Cow Bu-cola

Well now, there once lived in Iceland an old man and an old woman. They had a bit of a cottage, and a bit of a field, and they had one son, called Karl, and one cow, called Bu-cola, and that was all they had.

So, on a sunny morning, the old woman took her milking pail and her stool, and went out into the field to milk cow Bu-cola. But oh, dear me, cow Bu-cola wasn't there! The old woman ran about searching here, searching there; but she couldn't find cow Bu-cola anywhere. So she ran in home to the old man.

'Old man, old man, cow Bu-cola's vanished!'

The old man went and looked. The lad Karl went and looked. They searched here, they searched there, but they couldn't find cow Bu-cola. The old woman began to cry, the old man began to groan; so then Karl said, 'Mother, give me some new shoes and a knapsack full of bread and meat. I'm going out into the world to look for cow Bu-cola, and I'm not coming home until I've found her.'

Well, Karl got his new shoes and his knapsack full of bread and meat, and he set out. He walked long, long, searching and calling. But he couldn't find cow Bu-cola. And he felt tired and hungry, so he sat on a mossy stone to rest and eat.

And when he had eaten, he stood up and shouted with all his might, 'Moo now, my Bu-cola, moo if you are still alive!'

Did he hear? Yes, he did hear – far, far, and faint, faint – cow Bu-cola mooing.

So he walked on. He walked long, long. And again he felt tired and hungry, and again he sat down to rest and eat. And again, when he had eaten, he stood up and called, 'Moo now, my Bu-cola, moo, since you are still alive!'

What did he hear? He heard cow Bu-cola mooing; and the moo this time was a little nearer and a little louder. So he walked on.

He went long, long; he came to a great gorge, and on the edge of the gorge he sat down to rest and eat. And when he had eaten, he stood up and called again, 'Moo now, my Bu-cola, moo, since you are still alive!'

And cow Bu-cola moo'd, and the sound came from under his feet.

So he climbed down into the gorge, by a steep and winding path, and came into a big cave. He went into the cave, and what did he see? He saw cow Bu-cola, with a rope round her neck, tied to a peg in the cave wall.

'Oh, my cow Bu-cola! Oh, my cow Bu-cola!' Karl kissed cow Bu-cola on the nose. Then he untied the rope from the peg, led her up the steep and winding path out of the gorge, and set off for home.

Well, he hadn't gone very far when he heard a *clump, clump* of heavy feet behind him. He looked round – what did he see? He saw a huge troll wife striding after him, with a little troll girl running at her side.

'Oh me!' said Karl. 'What shall we do now, my Bu-cola?'

And cow Bu-cola answered, 'Pull a hair out of my tail, and lay it on the ground behind us.'

76

Well, Karl did that, and cow Bu-cola said, 'I magic, I magic and say, "Oh, hair out of my tail, become a great deep river that no one can cross, except a flying bird." '

And when cow Bu-cola said those words, the hair became a gigantic river, flowing between them and the troll wife.

The troll wife stood on the farther bank of the river and screamed out, 'That won't help you, you scoundrel!' And she sent the little troll girl home to fetch her great ox.

Karl and cow Bu-cola hurried on. But by and by back came the little troll galloping on the great ox. The ox put down his head and drank up all the river. Then he went home again, and the troll wife and the troll girl came clumping on.

'Oh me!' said Karl. 'What shall we do now, dear Bu-cola?'

And cow Bu-cola answered, 'Pull another hair out of my tail and lay it on the ground behind us.'

Well, Karl did that, and cow Bu-cola said, 'I magic, I magic and say, "Oh, hair out of my tail, become a great fire that nothing can pass over, not even a flying bird." '

And the hair became a fire that blazed from earth to heaven.

'This won't help you, you scoundrel!' screamed the troll wife.

And she sent the little troll girl home again to fetch the great ox.

The great ox came, he spat out all the river water he had swallowed, he quenched the fire.

And the troll wife came striding on.

'Oh me, oh me!' cried Karl. 'What shall we do now, dear Bu-cola?'

And cow Bu-cola answered, 'Pull yet a third hair out of my tail, and lay it on the ground behind us.'

Karl did that, and cow Bu-cola said, 'I magic, I magic and say "Oh hair out of my tail, become such a great mountain as none can get over, not even a flying bird." '

Then the hair became a mountain, so big, so high that you could see nothing to this side of it, nor to that side of it, and nothing above it save the blue of heaven.

'That won't help you, you scoundrel!' roared the troll wife from behind the mountain. And she sent the little troll girl home for her father's rock drill.

The little troll girl ran, she fetched the rock drill, she brought it to the troll wife. The troll wife began to bore through the mountain. She bored, bored, bored; she bored a hole right through the mountain. Then she began to creep through the hole. But the hole was too narrow for her great body, and half way through the mountain she stuck. She could neither go forward nor backward; she filled up the hole with her great body, and there she stuck, stuck, stuck. And by and by she turned to stone.

So on went Karl merrily, merrily, and brought cow Bu-cola home. The old woman clapped her hands, the old man danced a jig. Karl laughed, cow Bu-cola moo'd. There was great rejoicing in their bit of a cottage.

9. The Green Bird

The young princess Marvizia had a little rose tree in a pot. And every year that rose tree had just one flower. Marvizia never picked this flower; but when it withered and produced a hip, she picked the hip and ate it. For that rose hip was sweeter than honey, and the taste of it headier than wine. But one year there came a beautiful green bird, and it perched on the rose tree and ate the hip. Marvizia tried to catch the bird; it fluttered round her beating its wings – wings that glittered in the sun like green jewels; but no, it wouldn't let Marvizia catch it. And by and by it flew away.

Marvizia ran in crying (she was rather spoilt, you see) 'I want the Green Bird! I want the Green Bird!'

'Well, if it comes again next year, you must set a snare and catch it,' said the king, Marvizia's father.

'But I shall have to wait a whole year!' pouted Marvizia.

Now, strange to say, Marvizia hadn't to wait for a whole year. Something happened that had never happened before: next day there was another flower on the little rose tree; and by noon the rose had withered and had left behind it another glowing red hip.

Marvizia sent quickly for a bird catcher, and the bird catcher set a snare that would fall and catch the bird, should he alight on the tree. And, sure enough, the Green Bird came. But his eyes were bright, and his wits were sharp, and he saw the snare and wasn't caught in it. He hovered for a moment over the little rose tree, and then cried out, 'Alas, alas! She has set a snare for me! Now I will never come to her again.' And he flew off.

Marvizia shed tears. She went about crying, 'I want the Green Bird! I want the Green Bird!' And the king got angry and said, 'Then go and look for it.'

Of course, the king only said that because Marvizia was vexing him; he didn't mean her to go. But Marvizia did go. She put on a long black robe, and a hat with a cockle shell in it, such as pilgrims wear, and she took a staff in her hand, and set out.

She went, went, and all the time she was looking this way and that for a sight of the Green Bird, or for the sight of someone who might give her news of him. But she saw nothing, and she met nobody. So she came into a forest; and now it was night, and she saw a little hut and knocked at the door.

It was an old hermit who opened the door, and Marvizia said, 'Little father, have you seen the Green Bird passing this way?'

'Yes, little daughter,' said the hermit, 'the Green Bird passed this way three hours ago. But you can't go searching for him in the dark. Come in and rest till morning.'

So Marvizia went in, and the old hermit gave her food and shook down straw for her to sleep on. And in the morning, when she was ready to set out once more, he said, 'Little daughter, a hermit is not rich in this world's goods, but such as I have I will give you.' And he handed her a piece of wax. 'Keep it carefully,' said he, 'for, who knows, some day it may be of use.'

Marvizia didn't see what use a piece of wax would be to her; but she put the wax in the pocket of her robe, thanked the hermit, and went on her way. All day she was going, and in the evening came to a city where there was a palace draped in black.

'Why is the palace draped in black?' said she to the sentinel at the gate.

The sentinel said, 'Because the queen mourns for her son who is lost.'

Marvizia said, 'I am on pilgrimage, and I seek shelter for the night.'

The sentinel said, 'I will ask the queen, for she is merciful.'

So he went to ask the queen, and the queen said, 'Bring her to me.'

Now Marvizia was very beautiful, and when the queen saw her, she thought, 'If I had a daughter I would wish her to be like this young pilgrim!' And she had Marvizia to dine with her, and questioned her. But Marvizia only said, 'I am a poor pilgrim, your majesty, and I go to seek something I have lost.' But what that something was, Marvizia would not say.

Well, that night Marvizia got a soft bed. And in the morning the queen said, 'Little daughter, before you go, I would give you something to keep in remembrance of a sad queen, whose heart you have lightened by your presence.' And she took Marvizia into her treasure chamber and showed her many jewels, and said, 'Come choose; you shall have anything you fancy.'

Marvizia looked from one jewel to another jewel. She saw a gold ring set with a single diamond, and said, 'I would choose this ring.'

But the queen said, 'Alas, that I cannot give you, for it belongs to my son who is lost.'

Now it seemed to Marvizia that have that ring she must, and she begged the queen just to lend it to her, promising that on her return journey she would give it back. And she begged so prettily that the queen said, 'Well, take it, little one; but it is only a loan, not a gift.' And she put the ring on Marvizia's finger. And Marvizia said goodbye to the queen and went on her way.

She went, went, and at sunset came into a wide, flat, barren country, where there was just one steep hill. On the top of the hill was a castle, and she went up to the castle and knocked at the door. But when the door opened, she got a fright, for standing there was a huge black giant

'Oh, go away, go away, little lady,' said the huge black giant. 'This castle belongs to an ogress and she devours all who pass by.'

Marvizia would have fled, but just then the ogress came striding up the hill. In two steps she was at the door.

'Ali,' bawled the ogress to the black giant, 'put on the pot that I may boil this girl for supper.'

But Ali said, 'I have roasted two oxen and ten sheep, and boiled a pudding that weighs half a ton. Let the girl live till tomorrow – she is but a mouthful.'

So the ogress let Marvizia live. But she made Ali lock her in the cellar that she might not escape.

And in the morning the ogress said, 'Ali, put on the pot, that I may boil the girl for my breakfast.'

But Ali said, 'I have already cooked your breakfast. Don't eat the girl today. She is very thin. Keep her and feed her well, and when she is nice and plump, then eat her. Meanwhile she can help me with my work.'

The ogress said, '*That* girl will be of no use to you in your work!'

Ali said, 'How do you know that?'

The ogress said, 'I can tell by her niminy ways.'

Ali said, 'Give her a trial.'

The ogress said, 'Very well. Let her clean all my copper pots.

83

I'm going out. And if the pots are not all cleaned by the time I come back, I *will* eat her!'

Then the ogress stamped away down the hill, and Ali let Marvizia out of the cellar. He gave her a bite to eat, and then he took her into the kitchen, and showed her the copper pots. There were dozens of them, and they were all green with mould, and big as houses.

'Oh me, how am I to clean all those?' cried Marvizia.

'You can but try,' said Ali.

Marvizia began to weep. She looked out of the window. What did she see down there – down there at the bottom of the hill? She saw the Green Bird, perched on a bush of myrtle.

'Oh, my Green Bird! My Green Bird!'

'I will go and ask him how to clean the pots,' said Ali. And he strode away down the hill.

One stride down the hill; one stride up again. 'The Green Bird says, "Tell her to throw the wax the hermit gave her in the fire".'

Marvizia took the wax out of her pocket and threw it in the fire. What happened? Out of the fire came a crowd of giants with cloths, and brushes, and huge boxes of polish. They set to work on the copper pots; they had them clean and shining in no time. But when the work was finished – would they go back into the fire? No, they wouldn't. There they stood, all staring at Marvizia, and crowding up the kitchen.

'Thank you, thank you!' said Marvizia. 'But please go now.'

But the giants only stood and stared at her.

'I will go and ask the Green Bird how to get rid of them,' said Ali.

One stride down the hill, one stride up again. 'The Green Bird says, "Throw water on the fire".'

Marvizia took a little bucket of water, Ali took a huge bucket of water. *Swoosh!* They threw the water on the fire; the fire went out. And the giants went out with it.

By and by back came the ogress. She saw the copper pots all glittering like mirrors. They shone so brightly that she could see her ugly face in them, and that didn't please her. But she couldn't say the pots weren't clean. So she roared at Marvizia. 'You didn't do this without someone's help! But there, we'll talk of it tomorrow. Are you hungry?'

'I am a little,' said Marvizia.

'Then here's your dinner,' growled the ogress. And she gave Marvizia a great lump of raw meat, and stamped off.

Marvizia couldn't eat the meat. She went to the window to throw it out. What did she see down there – down on the plain? She saw the Green Bird dancing and singing. And the sight cheered her.

Then Ali brought her some apples and some bread, and said, 'Eat quickly. Hide the pips and stalks under the mat, and don't tell my mistress.'

So Marvizia ate, and was satisfied.

That evening the ogress again locked Marvizia in the cellar, and next morning dragged her up into the kitchen again.

'Girl,' says she, 'I'm not going to eat you, because I believe you are a witch, and witch meat lies heavy on the stomach. But I will have mincemeat made of you, all the same. Look down out of the window – what do you see?'

'I see a great barren plain stretching away and away,' said Marvizia, 'and I see herds of cattle moving on the plain.'

'Cattle?' snorted the ogress. 'Bulls, my girl, wild bulls. They have nothing to eat down there, because the grass is all dried up. They are raging mad! Oh ho! Won't they toss you on their horns, and trample you under their feet! Mincemeat you'll be when they've finished with you, yes, mincemeat! . . . Ali, take the baggage on your shoulders, and carry her down amongst the bulls. And won't you have a merry time there, my girl! Oh ho! Won't you!'

And off stamped the ogress, roaring with laughter.

'Ali, Ali, you can't, you won't do this!' cried Marvizia.

Ali said, 'I am under a spell, I have to obey her. But I will first go down and ask the Green Bird how we shall manage this affair.'

One stride down the hill; one stride up again. 'The Green Bird says to give me the ring from your finger. And fear nothing.'

So Marvizia gave Ali the ring. And Ali took her on his shoulders, carried her to the sun-scorched barren plain, and set her down. Then came the herd of wild bulls: like scarecrows they were, with their bones sticking up through their flesh. They came heads down, galloping sideways, bellowing with rage. But Ali held up the ring and said, 'Command! Command! Let the plain be covered with fresh green grass!' And lo, what had been sun-scorched barren earth was now fair green meadowland, stretching away and away into the distance. And the wild bulls were eagerly cropping the fresh green grass – they took no notice of Marvizia.

A stream, bordered by willows, ran through this fair green meadowland, and Ali set Marvizia down among the willows.

'The Green Bird bade me leave these things with you,' said he. And he took from his pocket bread and cheese and fruit and a bottle of wine. Then he went away and left her. Marvizia stayed for eight days hidden under the willows; she ate when she was hungry, and neither the food nor the wine decreased. The wild bulls came to drink at the stream, and they were friendly, for they thought that it was Marvizia who had brought them the green pasture.

But on the eighth day the ogress said to herself, 'I will go and see if there are any little bones left of that girl; if there are, I will make them into soup.' And she came tramping down out of the castle. She did not see the green grass, nor the stream. She saw what she wanted to see – and that was barren earth.

Now before she reached the plain, she had to pass through a little meadow, where a shepherdess was tending her sheep. And the shepherdess (lest she be eaten herself) had prepared a great feast for the ogress: roasted mutton by the hundredweight, an enormous loaf, and two barrels of wine. So the ogress sat down and ate and drank herself full, and what with the wine and the pleasant feeling of being stuffed with food, she shed a few enormous tears, and said, 'No one ever had compassion on me until now. But you have had compassion, and you shall marry my son.' For she called the Green Bird her son; though, as you may have guessed, he was the son of the sad queen; and the ogress had stolen him and turned him into a bird.

The ogress now picked up the shepherdess between the finger and thumb of her great hand, and carried her up to the castle. Then she called the Green Bird to her, gave him a slap and said, 'Become a man!' And at once, there he stood, a handsome prince.

The ogress gave the shepherdess a slap, and she gave the prince another slap, and said, 'Be you two husband and wife' – and that was all the marriage ceremony.

But Ali, unknown to anyone, had given the prince the ring of command, and up in the room where the prince and his bride were to sleep, he had laid a little trail of gunpowder at the foot of the bed. So the prince and the shepherdess went up to the room, each carrying a candle. And the prince put the candles on the floor at the foot of the bed, and began to undress very, very slowly. The candles burned down and down, and the shepherdess said, 'If you are not quicker we shall be left in the dark,' when all at once –

BANG! The candles had burned down to the gunpowder; room, bed, shepherdess and prince were all blown sky-high, and whirled away down on to the plain.

What became of the shepherdess we are not told; but the prince picked himself up and ran, ran, to the place where Marvizia was hidden under the willows, and he took her by the hand, and they ran, ran – and there was Ali striding along behind them.

But the ogress was after them, and for every yard that they ran, she ran three, so the prince held up the ring of command, and said, 'Let there be a tower of bronze here, and ourselves in the turrets!' And there they were, all three, up on the top of a high bronze tower, with the ogress standing down below and biting herself with rage.

Then the prince held up the ring again, and said, 'Command! Command! Let the ogress become solid gold, and sink twenty roods under the earth.' And the ogress stood there turned into a huge gold statue, and she sank down, and down, and down, into the earth. And the earth covered her.

Then the prince held up the ring once more, and said, 'Command! Command! Let this plain become a rich kingdom filled with happy people, and let there be a city in the midst of the kingdom, and in the city a princely palace, with manservants and maidservants, and gardens and orchards, and stables, and horses and carriages.'

And at once, there it all was, just as the prince had commanded. So the prince and Marvizia and Ali went into the palace.

Marvizia stripped off her pilgrim's dress and bathed in scented water, and arrayed herself in such beautiful garments as became a princess.

The prince said, 'Go, Marvizia, and bring the queen, my mother, to me.'

Then Marvizia set out in a golden coach and came to the sad queen's palace, and began taking down the black mourning cloths.

The queen said, 'Who are you that you take down the mourning cloths I have set up for my lost son?'

And Marvizia answered, 'Do you not know me, my queen? I am the little pilgrim to whom you gave your son's ring. And now you must mourn no longer for your son who was lost is found. But I cannot return the ring, for your son wears it.'

And she told the queen the whole story.

Then the queen rejoiced. She got into the golden coach and drove with Marvizia to the prince's palace.

What need to tell of the gladness of that meeting? What need to tell, either, of the magnificence of the next day's wedding between the prince and Marvizia? But there is one thing more that shall be told.

After the wedding, the prince went out into the city square, held up the ring and said, 'Command! Command! Let there come forth fifty giants, and let them go and dig the ogress out of the ground.'

And the giants came, and they dug down into the earth, and pulled up the great gold statue of the ogress. They put it on a huge wagon, yoked all the wild bulls to the wagon, brought the statue into the city, and set it up in the square outside the palace. Very splendid it looked there, shining in the sun; and the people said, 'See how she glitters! And nobody need fear her any more!'

Then the queen went back to her own kingdom; Marvizia and the prince ruled happily over *their* kingdom; and Ali, the good black giant, stayed with them, and served them faithfully all his life.

10. Jon and the Troll Wife

Once upon a time, far away in the north of the world, there lived a peasant farmer. The country where this man lived was small, and it was surrounded by the sea. The man's wife was long dead, and he had an only son – a lad called Jon. In the spring and summer Jon and his father worked in their little fields. In autumn they packed their fishing gear into an old wagon, harnessed in their two horses, locked up their little house, and set off for the western islands to fish. And in these western islands they stayed fishing all through the autumn and winter; and only came back to their little farm in time for the spring sowing of wheat.

But one autumn the man fell sick, and he said to his son, 'My lad, I can't travel to the islands this year – you must go alone. Now listen carefully to what I say. You know that the road you must take passes under the mountains. And as you drive along under the mountains, you will come to a high overhanging rock, black and glittering. As you value your life, do not linger near that rock, for it is the haunt of the trolls. And by offending the trolls, or trying to pry into their affairs, many a good man has come to his death. Now, go on your way; and my blessing go with you, dear son.'

So Jon bade his father goodbye and set out. He drove all day, and at dusk he was still going along under the mountains. He was tired, and his two horses, poor things, were stumbling with weariness. To make matters worse, a frightful storm arose. The wind howled, lightning flashed, thunder boomed, the rain pelted down. Jon looked for shelter, but found none. Then suddenly, as a flash of lightning lit up the stony road and the towering mountains, he saw, close beside him, a high overhanging rock, black and glittering: a shelter as fine as could be wished, rich with grass underfoot, and the great rock itself a bastion over one's head from both wind and rain.

Jon forgot his father's warning; he drove the cart in under the rock, unharnessed the horses, tethered them, and left them to crop the grass, while he himself unpacked his food hamper, and sat down to supper.

Well, suddenly, while he was eating, but long before his hunger was satisfied, there came from somewhere farther back under the rock – where in the dusk he could just make out the mouth of a cave – a tremendous howling: one voice and another voice howling together, 'We want food! *We want food! WE WANT FOOD!*'

'Well, you shall have it!' shouted Jon. And he took a big fish from his hamper, split it open, spread the two halves with butter, carried them to the cave mouth, tossed them in, and shouted, 'Here's something for you!'

Immediately the howling stopped, and all was quiet.

Jon finished his supper; and as it was now dark, he was about to wrap himself in a horse cloth and lie down to sleep when he heard, coming along the road outside his shelter, a *scrunch, scrunch, scrunch* of heavy footsteps. Someone came to the rock shelter, someone came in under it: a huge troll wife, whose body shone all over in the darkness with little lights – a sight which turned our Jon faint with terror – while her great voice rumbled under the rock walls, 'A human smell in my hole! I smell a man in my hole!'

And she strode past him and flung a bundle she was carrying *flump* into the cave, making the cave walls boom and rattle.

By and by, back she came again carrying a lighted candle. And Jon plucked up heart, for he saw that her face, though scarred like the very mountains themselves into deep ruts and wrinkles, was not unkindly. In fact, her huge mouth was widened in a friendly grin.

'I thank you for feeding my children,' said she. 'Come!' And she picked him up, tucked him under her arm, and carried him into the cave.

Inside the cave were two great beds, and in one of the beds lay two troll children. ('Ah! It must have been those two who were howling,' thought Jon.) And on the floor of the cave lay a huge heap of trout in a great net. ('Ah! It was that net full of trout she was carrying that made her shine in the dark!' thought Jon.)

'You shall have a bed,' boomed the troll wife. 'Which bed will you have – mine or the children's?'

'I can sleep quite comfortably on the ground,' said Jon.

'No, a bed! A bed!' roared the troll wife. 'Come, which bed?'

So then Jon said he would have the children's bed. And the troll wife lifted up the sleeping children, and set them gently on the ground. Then Jon climbed up into the children's bed, and immediately fell asleep.

In the morning he woke to feel himself being lifted out of bed by the troll wife. She set him on the sandy floor of the cave, and brought him a breakfast of fried trout. 'The sun shines, the wind has dropped, the storm is over,' she boomed. 'You can go safely on your way. But where are you going?'

So Jon told her, and she said, 'Have you arranged for a place in one of the fishing boats?'

93

'No,' said Jon. 'I must take my chance.'

'Then I will tell you how it is,' said she. 'All the places in the boats are already taken; and on the isthmus from which the boats set out every day for the fishing grounds, all the lodgings are filled, except in the cabin of a very old fisherman, whose boat leaks like a sieve. No skilled fisherman will go into partnership with that old man, for he has had no luck for years But you shall go into partnership with him, and you shall lodge in his cabin. It is time his luck turned, and turn it shall. Here are two fish hooks: one for you, and one for the old fisherman. You must use these hooks and no others, and you and he must do your fishing alone. Every morning, wait until all the other boats have set off before you row out. And always return before the other boats in the evening. Row no farther than the rock nearest the landing place, and there throw out your lines. Now do you understand, and will you do as I say?'

'I will do as you say,' said Jon.

'Well, then,' said she, 'when you come to the isthmus, tether your horses on the sand. Don't ask anyone to see to them. *I* will see to them through the winter. And in the spring I will send my own horse to join yours, for I think you will spare a few dried fish for my horse to bring me?'

'I will do all that you tell me, and all that you ask of me,' said Jon.

'You won't regret it,' said she. 'Now be off! I've filled your hamper for you.' And she laughed her huge laugh, picked Jon up, and put him outside the cave.

So Jon untethered his two horses, harnessed them, hitched them up to the cart, and went on his way. He came to the isthmus where the fishermen had their winter lodgings and their sheds for drying the fish. He found everything just as the troll wife had told him: all the lodgings were taken, all the places in the fishing boats were

94

filled. The fishermen were friendly enough; but when they saw Jon unharness his two horses and tether them on the sand, they laughed at him for a crazy loon.

'And what do you propose to do next, young fellow,' said they, 'since all the places in the boats are filled?'

'I think there is yet one place vacant,' said Jon. And he went to seek out the old unlucky fisherman, and said he wished to go into partnership with him.

'Go into partnership with *me!*' shrilled the old man. 'No, no, that can't be! I won't take you! I have no luck! My boat leaks! I never catch fish! You might as well go into partnership with the devil himself!'

'Well, then,' said Jon, 'give me a lodging for the night.'

The old man wasn't willing even to do that. But at last he said that Jon could sleep on the kitchen floor. 'And in the morning you best way harness up and turn home again,' said he.

'The morning is wiser than the evening,' said Jon. 'We'll leave it at that.'

So he shared his supper with the old man. It was a very good supper – the troll wife had seen to that when she packed his hamper – and Jon soon had the old man chuckling and smacking his lips. Indeed he was so grateful that he wanted Jon to share his bed; but Jon said no, the floor was good enough for him. So they slept through the night, and woke to see all the boats rowing out to the fishing grounds in beautiful calm weather.

'Now you best pack up and go home,' said the old man.

'Show me your boat first,' said Jon.

The old man took him down to the harbour. There the boat lay on her side above the water line. No beauty certainly! Old, battered, and half full of water.

'Let's run her down into the sea,' said Jon.

'No, no, she leaks!' screamed the old man.

'That's soon put right,' said Jon. And he fetched tar and rags and pieces of cork, and caulked the holes in her, and ran her down into the water, while the old man stood watching him, and wringing his hands.

'I've a mind to row her out a little way,' said Jon, 'Coming?'

The old man wouldn't, he wouldn't, he *wouldn't!* But Jon talked him round, and by and by he got into the boat, sighing and moaning; and Jon took the oars and they pushed off. The boat wasn't leaking. She was riding the water like a bird, and they soon reached the rock that was nearest the landing place.

'Now,' said Jon, 'for fun we'll throw in our lines. I've two hooks here, one for me and one for you.' And he fastened one hook to his line, baited it, and cast it into the water.

Tug, tug, tug: in one moment he pulled in a fish.

He baited his hook again, cast his line again. *Tug, tug, tug!* Immediately another fish. And when the old man, all excited, took the other hook, fastened it to a line, baited it, and threw it over-

board, the same thing happened. They pulled in fish after fish, till very soon the boat was loaded down. They rowed back to shore, cleaned the fish, and hung them up to dry.

It was still early in the day, so they set out for the rock again, and caught another boat-load of fish, and rowed back to land with them, and cleaned them, and hung them up to dry. And again set out, and again filled the boat, and were back with their third load long before the rest of the fishermen returned.

And when the fishermen saw Jon's catch, they were amazed. Where had he found so many fish?

Jon told them, and next morning all the boats were fishing round that rock, but they caught nothing. So they rowed farther out. And when they were all gone from sight, Jon and the old man rowed to the rock again, and filled their boat three times over, just as they had the day before. And so it went on all through the autumn and all through the winter. The old man wasn't moaning and groaning any more: he was laughing from morning to night.

So came the last day of the fishing season. And on that day, when Jon and the old man rowed out to the rock, and cast their lines, something gave a tug and pulled the lines deep down into the water. And when they pulled them in again, both the hooks were gone, as if they had been cut off.

So they rowed home.

Now all the fishermen were teasing Jon about his horses, which he had tethered on the sand. 'They'll be in fine fettle to carry your load of fish home!' said they. 'They must be skin and bone by now, if they haven't dropped down dead! Likely enough you'll find the crows picking their carcases!'

'I don't think so,' said Jon. 'But we'll go and see.'

So they went to the sands, and the men followed him. What did they see? Jon's horses securely tethered, and fatter than ever. And beside them a huge brown horse, carrying a pack saddle.

The men were frightened. 'The lad must be a wizard,' said they. And they fell silent, and left him.

Jon loaded up the huge brown horse with as much fish as the horse could carry, and that was more than a lot. And the rest of his fish he piled into the wagon, harnessed up his own two horses, and set off merrily on his way home. He came to the great rock, and found the troll wife on the look out for him.

'I took my fish-hooks back,' said she, in her booming voice. And there they were, dangling from her great hand. 'I looked after your horses well, too, and I brought my own to join them. Now, what have you brought me?'

'As much fish as the horse could carry,' said Jon. 'But if you wish for more, you shall take what you will from the wagon.'

'And send you home empty-handed?' said the troll wife. 'No, no, Jon, we'll do better than that! But you shall stay with me for a couple of days before you go home; for I have much to tell you.'

So Jon stayed, and she told him that all the trolls had left that part of the country: that her husband had come and gone again, taking the children with him. And that she had only waited to say goodbye before she too set out.

'And so you will never see me again, Jon,' said she. 'Except in a dream. But one night this spring you will dream of me, and then you will know that I have gone. Then you must come back to the cave, and all that you find here will be yours – a parting present from an old troll wife, whose children you fed when they were hungry. And now off with you to your father, my lad, for he's wearying for news of you. But don't forget the old troll wife, Jon!'

'How could I ever forget you?' said Jon.

Then the troll wife gave such a laugh that the cave walls boomed and rattled. She picked up Jon with one hand and put him outside the cave.

Jon harnessed the two horses to the wagon, and drove off home with his great load of fish. He found his father completely recovered and overjoyed to see him, though he shook his head over Jon's having ignored his warning about the great rock. Yes, he had to admit that it all turned out wonderfully well; but then, oh dear, it mightn't have!

Now whether it was a short time, or whether it was a long time after that, I can't tell you; but one night Jon had a dream. He dreamed that he saw the troll wife standing outside his father's little house, so huge, so huge that her head blotted out the stars. And in the morning he said, 'Father, I am going away for a day, or maybe two days. And though my errand is urgent, I scarce can tell what I seek, or what I may find. But you shall know of it when I return.'

'Then go with my blessing, my son,' said the father. And Jon set out on horseback. He rode, rode, along under the mountains till he came to the overhanging rock, black and glittering.

'Troll wife!' he called. But he got no answer, save the echo of his own voice. So he dismounted and went in under the rock.

What did he see? He saw two boulders, and on each boulder stood a big crate. The crates were bound round with chains; on the lid of each crate was an iron ring, and beside each ring lay a coil of rope.

There was a paper, too, nailed to the lid of each crate. The papers had the words scrawled on them in great black letters: and the words said, 'For Jon from the troll wife.' And as Jon stood gazing at the crates, and wondering how he could even lift them, much less carry them home, a shadow fell behind him, and there was the great brown horse coming in under the rock.

'Jon,' said the great brown horse, 'my mistress has sent me. It is I who will carry the crates home for you.'

The great brown horse had his pack saddle on his back, and he went to stand between the boulders. Now all that Jon had to do was to pass the ropes through the rings on the crates, and fasten the ropes one on each side of the great horse's pack saddle. Then out on to the road with them, and Jon up on his own horse, and riding slowly back home, with the great brown horse following behind him.

When Jon got home, he and his father opened the crates. What did they find? Bars of gold, bars of silver, diamonds and rubies, precious gems of all kinds, brought by the troll wife from her treasure house among the mountains. Now they were rich. They lived in peace and plenty, blessing the troll wife every day of their lives.

And the great brown horse went back to his mistress.

11. The Little Tailor and the Three Dogs

Once upon a time a little tailor lived in a little town where he found but little work. So one day he put a clean shirt and a piece of bread in his knapsack, slung the knapsack over his shoulder, took his yardstick in his hand, and off with him to seek a larger town where he might find more work.

Well, his way led him into a great dark forest; and there he was, marching along and singing, when a great big dog jumped out from behind the trees.

'Good day, little tailor,' says the great big dog, wagging his tail. 'Will you take me with you?'

'As to that,' says the little tailor, 'I should be glad of your company. But what to feed you on – well there, that's the problem. For though I *had* a bit of bread, I've just eaten every scrap of it.'

'Trust me, I can find food,' says the great big dog.

'Oh ho, can you so?' says the little tailor. 'Then I'll take you, if you'll run behind and be obedient.'

'That I will!' says the great big dog.

'Forward *march* then!' says the little tailor.

And on they go, and on they go, the little tailor in front, whistling and singing, and the great big dog running at his heels.

Well, they hadn't gone far, when another great big dog came jumping out from behind the trees.

'Good day, little tailor,' says this second great big dog wagging his tail. 'Will you take me with you?'

'Truly,' says the little tailor, 'I've already got one dog too many. But, yes, if you'll be obedient, you can run behind and keep my first dog company.'

'I will be obedient, master,' says the second big dog.

And on they go, and on they go, the little tailor singing and whistling, and the two dogs running behind.

Well now, would you believe it – before they'd gone all that far, what should come jumping out from behind the trees but a third big dog.

'Good day, little tailor,' says the third big dog, wagging his tail. 'Will you take me with you?'

'Truly,' says the little tailor, 'I've heard tell that all good things come in threes. So if you will be obedient, you can run behind with the other two.'

'Yes, I will be obedient, master,' says the third dog.

So on they go and on they go, the little tailor whistling and singing, and the three dogs running behind.

By and by they came out of the forest. There now was a village, and the first house in the village was a tavern, with a board on a pole swinging over the door. The board had words written on it; GOOD FOOD FOR MAN AND BEAST.

The little tailor looked up at the board and sighed. 'We are all four hungry,' said he. 'But what a shilling looks like I have long since forgotten.'

'Is that all, master?' says the first big dog. 'You go inside. Order meat and drink for four, and never worry about the reckoning. *We'll* see to that.'

'Well, if you say so,' answered the little tailor. 'Courage, my heart!' And he swung his yardstick three times round his head. 'Here goes!' says he, and marches into the tavern, bangs with his fist on a table, and when the host comes running, orders a meal for four, the best in the house, with boiled meat and roast meat, and wine and beer. He throws his knapsack and his hat on a bench, stands his yardstick up in a corner, and seats himself in an armchair.

The host laid the table for four, brought in the boiled and the roast, the wine and the beer; and no sooner was the food on the table than the door flew open and in rushed the three dogs. Each one sprang on to a chair and began to eat and drink; and if they had been human beings they couldn't have behaved better.

Was the host astonished? He was! He struck his hands together and cried out, 'Lord save us!'

So when the four of them had eaten all the food, and drunk all the wine and beer, the first dog said to the little tailor, 'Now be off with you, master, as fast as your legs can carry you. Leave everything lying here.'

The little tailor made off, leaving his hat and his knapsack on the bench, and his yardstick standing in the corner.

So, seeing the hat and the knapsack and the yardstick, the host thought the little tailor had just gone out for a breath of air, and would surely soon be back again; and he carried away the empty dishes into the kitchen. But no sooner was his back turned than the first dog seized up the hat, the second dog seized up the knapsack, the third dog seized up the yardstick, and off they scampered after the little tailor.

'I doubt we're but four rascals,' says the little tailor. 'But there, folk must eat.'

And they all doubled back into the forest.

'Now *I* shall lead the way,' said the first big dog, running on in front.

They went, went, went, and they came to a clearing. And in the clearing stood a great castle.

'Have you any courage, my master?' says the first dog.

'A deal more courage than cash,' says the little tailor.

'Well, then,' says the first dog, 'tie us all three to one cord.'

'I don't know that I have a cord,' says the little tailor.

'Look in your knapsack,' says the first dog.

The little tailor looked in his knapsack. Sure enough, coiled up inside it was a length of cord. And he tied up the three dogs one behind the other.

'What now?' says he.

'You're going to lead us into the castle,' says the first big dog. 'You'll find plenty of ogres in it, and you must sell us to them. But don't trust them, for they're spiteful, wicked, cunning double-twisters. So, to protect you, we'll each give you a gift. Feel in my right ear.'

The little tailor felt in the first dog's right ear, and took out a pot of ointment.

'Good,' said the first dog. 'If you smear that ointment on a chair, whoever sits on the chair will stick fast.'

'Now feel in *my* right ear,' said the second dog.

The little tailor felt in the second dog's right ear, and took out a little stick.

'Good,' said the second dog. 'That stick looks short, but it will lengthen itself in need. And if you hit anybody on the head with it, that anybody will die.'

'Now feel in *my* right ear,' said the third dog.

The little tailor did so, and took out a little horn.

'Good,' said the third dog. 'When you need us, blow that horn, and we'll come.'

'Ah ha!' said the little tailor. 'But first I must see if I *can* blow it. After all this scurrying about, a body is short of breath.'

Well, he puts the horn to his lips and blows. What a clang! The castle walls echo, the castle door flies open, and the little tailor marches in, leading the three dogs behind him tied to the cord.

'Anyone at home?'

No answer.

They were in a great hall with a staircase at the back of it. So, seeing nobody, the little tailor, with the three dogs, went up the stairs and came into a huge room, where twenty-four huge ogres sat at a huge table, drinking out of twenty-four huge beakers.

The little tailor takes off his hat. Bows low. 'Would any of you gentlemen ogres like to buy three handsome dogs?'

'What's your price?' roared the ogre who sat at the head of the table – he was the biggest and ugliest of them all.

'Three gold pieces,' says the little tailor. 'And that's cheap enough.'

'Agreed,' says the ogre. 'You wait here; we'll go and put the dogs in the stable, and fetch the money.' He winked at the other ogres, and grinned and chuckled. And all the ogres winked, and they all grinned and chuckled. Then they went off with the dogs.

'Ho!' thinks the little tailor. 'Blows the wind out of that quarter? I'll spoil your fun!' And he climbed on to one chair after another and smeared each one with the sticky ointment, above, below, before, behind. There was enough ointment in that little pot to smear the whole world, had he wanted so to do.

Now, having chained up the dogs in the stable, the ogres were holding counsel together outside the room door. The tailor was small, granted, and the tailor was skinny; but better skinny human flesh than no human flesh at all. So they decided what they would say and all tramped back into the room.

'Tailor,' said the biggest ogre, looking very fierce, 'you have deceived us. Those dogs of yours aren't worth a penny. And having deceived us, you must die.'

'Gentlemen ogres,' said the little tailor, 'if I have deserved death, then I am willing to die. But no man is condemned without being heard. You should hold a trial and let me speak in my own defence.'

Ho, ho! The ogres thought that would be fun! They moved their chairs into a half circle, sat down, and bade the tailor sit on a stool facing them.

'Now begin your defence, earthworm!' said the biggest ogre.

'I begin, gentlemen ogres,' said the little tailor, 'by condemning you all to death.'

'Ha! ha! ha!' A roar of laughter went up from the ogres – they thought this was the biggest joke in the world.

'Nay, but I am serious,' said the little tailor. 'You needn't laugh. You would swindle me, would you? *I* deceive *you*, indeed! It is you who are trying to deceive me. But I will not be deceived, gentlemen ogres. You pay for my dogs, or else you die.'

And with that he got up from his stool and took a leap backwards, well out of reach of the ogres' long arms.

The ogres weren't laughing now; they were howling with rage. They were trying to get up from their chairs, but they were stuck fast. The little tailor waved his little stick; the stick grew longer and longer; the little tailor touched each ogre on the head with the stick, and one after another the ogres fell dead.

'Thank you, my stick,' said the little tailor. 'Now I can take a rest.'

Oh ho, could he take a rest? No, he couldn't. What was that noise he heard on the stairs? *Tramp, tramp! Tramp, tramp! TRAMP!* The walls shuddered, the door fell down, and in strode an ogre twice as big as any of the others, and twice as hideous – the ogre king, just returned from hunting.

'Who has done this?' roared the ogre king. 'Who has dared to kill my people?'

'I have dared, and I have done it,' said the little tailor.

'Too skinny to eat,' bawled the ogre king, 'too wicked to live! You shall be hung up in the garden to scare the birds!'

The little tailor tried to hit the ogre on the head with his stick; but the ogre seized the stick and broke it in two. He picked up the little tailor between his finger and thumb and carried him, kicking and biting, out into the garden. The ogre set the little tailor on the top of the highest tree, and took a rope from his pocket. 'Now we shall string you up!' he roared.

But the little tailor blew his horn; the horn gave a blast that echoed for miles and miles. 'That won't save you,' roared the ogre king. 'Who d'you think you're calling with your twopenny-ha'penny horn?'

'My dogs!' shouted the little tailor. 'And here they come!'

The three dogs came racing: they had broken chains round their necks. 'Master, come down from that tree!' cried the first dog.

'Come down! Come down!' cried the other two.

'How can I come down, my children?' said the little tailor. 'The ogre king is going to hang me.'

Then the three dogs turned on the ogre king. They leaped, they snarled, they bit, they tore; they soon had the ogre all in pieces.

'Master, now come down from that tree!' cried the first dog.

The little tailor climbed down. He looked about him in bewilderment. The dogs had disappeared – and what were those dark hairy things that were lying on the ground? Three dog skins! The little tailor stared. 'Strange things have been happening,' said he, 'but this is the strangest of all!'

Then he heard a voice calling from among the trees. 'Little tailor, little tailor, come here!'

'Well, I'm coming,' said the little tailor; 'but it seems to me

that these happenings are a bit too much! Yes, a bit too much,'
said he.

And he went in among the trees.

What did he see? He saw a king with a gold crown on his head.
He saw a queen with a gold crown on *her* head. And standing at
the queen's side, he saw the loveliest little princess in all the
world.

'Little tailor,' said the king, 'you are our deliverer. The ogre
king cast a spell on us and turned us into dogs, because we would
not give him our daughter in marriage. But now the enchantment
is broken. Come, let us go into the castle.'

In they went, and found the great hall thronged with courtiers.
The little tailor looked through the window. Would you believe
it? The forest was turning into a city, the little trees were turning
into houses, the big trees were turning into churches and towers,
the birds were turning into people going happily about their
business. And beyond the city on all sides there stretched a fair
and fertile country.

'It is you who have done all this for us,' said the princess. And
she put her two white hands on the little tailor's shoulders, and
kissed him on the lips.

That settled it – if it wasn't settled before. Next day there was
a merry wedding – the wedding of the little tailor and the princess.
And the first thing the little tailor did after the wedding was to
send for the host of the tavern, and pay him four times over for
the food he and the three dogs had eaten.

'Rascal when in need I may have been,' said the little tailor.
'But I would not keep a guilty conscience now that I am to live
in plenty.'

12. The Troll's Little Daughter

A handsome lad was walking from the south along a wide, empty road. And a big ugly troll was walking fom the north along the same road. And they two met, plumb, in the middle of the road.

Said the troll, 'Where are you going?'

Said the lad, 'To where I can find work.'

Said the troll, 'Come and work for me.'

Said the lad, 'All right.'

The lad knew he'd have to say 'all right' anyway, because a troll isn't a body you can say 'no' to, if you value your life.

'I give good wages,' said the troll. 'You shall have a bushel of gold at the end of your first year's service; two bushels of gold at the end of the second year; and three bushels of gold at the end of the third year.'

'Well, I call that handsome!' said the lad.

There was a great mound near by, and that was where the troll lived. The troll took the lad into the mound, and down and down and down underground, till they came to a stable. The stable was a mile long and a mile wide. In the stable the troll had tied up all the wild creatures of the forest: bears, foxes, hares, wolves, squirrels, and deer. And he had all the birds of the air caged up too.

'Your work is to feed my creatures,' said the troll. And he showed the lad a huge storeroom beyond the stable.

All that day the lad worked hard, he was at it till late at night, carrying meat for some animals, hay and corn, nuts and acorns for others, and seeds and insects for the birds. And pails and pails full of water. By the time he'd done all that, he was worn out, and he slumped down on a heap of straw and fell asleep.

In the morning the troll woke him, took him into a room, and gave him a good breakfast. 'You've done well, my lad,' said he. 'My creatures won't need feeding again for a while. So in the meantime I'll allow you to play.' And he said a strange word and turned the lad into a hare. 'Off with you into the forest,' says he.

How it happened the hare never knew; but there he was next minute, racing away under the forest trees.

Ah ha! And didn't that hare enjoy himself at first, leaping and running, and stopping to nibble the grass, and running again!

'What a slowcoach I used to be!' thought the hare. 'And now – see me run! See me run!'

Yes, that was all very well, but soon he found he *had* to run, whether he would or no; for he being the only animal left in the forest, all the huntsmen and all the dogs were after him. Bullets and arrows whizzed round him, and dogs ran yelping, and raced sniffing, along his tracks. But somehow or other no dog could catch up with him. And let the huntsmen shoot this way or that way, the hare, doubling in his tracks, and twisting and turning, and galloping on, always managed to outmanoeuvre them. It was a restless life, that it was! But the hare came to enjoy it, and to be proud of outwitting both huntsmen and dogs.

Well, it may have been a short time, but more like it was a long time, when one day the hare heard the troll calling. And next minute that hare was inside the mound again. The troll said his strange word (only he said it backwards this time), and the hare turned back into the lad.

'Now how do you like my service!' said the troll. 'And how did you enjoy being a hare?'

'It pleased me well,' said the lad. 'Never before could I run so swiftly, or leap so joyously.'

'Well then – here's your first year's wages,' said the troll.

And he gave the lad a bushel of gold.

Was the lad delighted? I tell you he was! And when the troll asked him if he would serve for another year, the lad said 'Oh *yes*!'

'Then go and feed my creatures,' said the troll.

The lad went down into the great stable. He worked hard all that day; and late at night he fell asleep quite worn out, as he had done the year before. And in the morning the troll woke him and gave him breakfast, and said. 'You've done well. Now you can go and play again.' And he said his strange word.

What happened this time? The lad turned into a raven, and flew up high, high above the forest. Oh, but that raven was delighted! The blue sky above him, the air so fresh and sweet, and himself flying strongly, and wheeling and soaring, and now and then doing those wonderful upside down tumbling dives that only ravens know how to perform.

No dogs to worry him, either! But there *was* something to worry him, none the less: for he being the only bird in the air (all the others having been caged by the troll) every huntsman in the neighbourhood was after him, and the guns banged away at him from morning to night. However, somehow or other the huntsmen could never hit him, and he came to enjoy dodging the bullets.

So, after what may have been a short time, but more likely was a long time, the raven heard the troll's voice calling him home. Next minute – there he was inside the mound again. And the troll said his strange word backwards, and turned the raven back into a lad.

'How do you like my service now?' said the troll. 'And how did you enjoy being a raven?'

'I enjoyed it mightily,' said the lad. 'Never before did I know the delight of flying through the air.'

'Well, here's your second year's pay,' said the troll. And he gave the lad two bushels of gold.

If the lad had been delighted with his first year's wages, he was doubly delighted with his second year's. And when the troll asked him if he was willing to serve for yet a third year, the lad said, 'Yes, *yes!*'

So down he went into the stable to feed the animals and birds. (And having known the delight of running and flying free, he felt sorry for those animals and birds.) He worked hard till late at night, and fell into a dreamless sleep on his bed of straw when his work was finished, and was shaken into wakefulness by the troll next morning, and given breakfast, for which he was rare and hungry.

Soon as the lad had eaten, the troll said, 'You can go and play again.' And he spoke the strange word, and turned the lad into a little silver fish.

There was the little silver fish, now, swimming in the stream that flowed past the troll's mound. And oh, how happy he was, darting to and fro under the cool water! The stream ran swiftly, and it carried the little fish farther and farther away, till it reached the sea. And the little fish went with the stream's waters into the great sea, and swam on and on and on.

What do you think? By and by that little fish came to a great glass palace standing on the bottom of the sea. The little fish swam round and round the palace. The glass was so clear, so clear, that he could see into all the rooms. What magnificence! The furniture was of white whalebone, inlaid with gold and pearls. There were curtains and cushions of all the colours of the rainbow, and beautiful carpets of green moss. Little sparkling fountains gushed babbling out of great white snail shells, and trickled away down silver pipes, filling the palace with the most charming music. But most charming of all was a little maiden, who was walking about all alone from one room to another room. The little fish had never seen anything more lovely than that little maiden; and yet she looked so sad: all the beautiful things surrounding her might have been so much trash, from the sadness with which she looked at them.

The little fish swam round and round the palace; but he had no eyes now for all the magnificence he saw there. He had eyes only for the maiden.

'What is the use of being a *fish*?' he thought. 'Oh, if I were but a lad again that I might speak with that maiden!'

Then he remembered the strange word that the troll had spoken to turn him from one shape into another shape. I can't tell you what the word was exactly. It was something like *zzzz yytpx* – and if you can say that, either forwards or backwards, it's more than I can. The troll had said it forwards to turn the lad into an animal, and backwards to turn him once more into a lad. So now the little fish had to say it backwards, and somehow he managed it. Then, in a moment, the little fish was gone, and there, standing on the bottom of the sea, was the lad. And the lad went into the palace to the maiden.

Was that little maiden startled? I tell you she was! But the lad told her all about himself, and how he had come there, and then she laughed and clapped her hands, and looked very, very happy.

'It was the troll who put me here,' she said. 'He calls me his little daughter. But I am not his daughter. I am *not*! I am the daughter of a king, and the troll stole me away, and brought me here so that none should find me. But *you* have found me, dear, dearest lad, and now I am not lonely any more!'

So they lived together in that palace under the sea for a whole year. When they were hungry a table spread itself with food for them. When they were weary, there were golden beds with silken draperies for them to sleep in. The hours flew by, the days flew by, the lad wished for nothing better than to stay down there with the princess all his life. But one day she said to him, 'Dear lad, the troll will soon be calling you back, and you must turn once more into a fish, or you will never get safely through the sea.'

'I can't leave you here alone, and I won't!' said the lad.

'Ah, but you must,' said the princess. 'And I have thought of a plan by which you may rescue me, if you will do exactly as I tell you.'

'I will do exactly as you tell me,' said the lad.

'Then you must leave the troll,' said the princess, 'and take service with my father, the king. But be sure to carry with you all the gold that the troll has given you. My father owes the troll money; he is soon due to pay his debts, and if he can't pay he will lose his head. Tell the king you will lend him the money on condition that he takes you with him when he goes to pay the troll. Disguise yourself as the king's fool, and when you come with the king to the troll's dwelling, act like a madman and do all the damage you can. Then the troll will fly into a rage. He will say that you and the king must lose your lives unless one of you can answer three questions. *You* will answer those questions.'

Then the princess told the lad what the questions would be, and how he must answer. And scarcely had she finished telling him when he heard the troll's voice, like a thousand rolling drums, sounding through the sea to call him home. The voice echoed through the glass palace, making the walls quiver and the fountains spatter their bright water over the green moss carpets.

'The word – the word!' cried the princess. 'Quick! Our lives depend on it!'

The lad didn't want to say the word – he wanted to stay where he was. But the princess got angry and slapped him, and then he said it. And at once – princess, palace and lad – everything vanished. Now there was only the little silver fish swimming fast, fast, through the sea, and up the stream towards the troll's mound.

The troll stood on the bank of the stream. He caught up the little fish in his great hand. He grunted out the word backwards. The little fish disappeared, and there stood the lad.

'Well,' said the troll, 'how did you like being a fish?'

'Oh, it pleased me best of all!' said the lad.

The troll took the lad into the mound and gave him three bushels of gold. Now altogether he had six bushels.

'If you'll serve me another year,' said the troll, 'I'll give you six bushels more. Then you'll have twelve.'

But the lad said he wanted to see something more of the world. And then I'll come back,' said he.

'You'll be welcome,' said the troll. 'You'll be welcome any time.'

So the lad took his six bushels of gold and set out for the country of the king who was the princess's father. It took him a long and weary time to get there, but get there he did in the end. He buried his gold in a field near the king's palace, and then he went to the king's stable and took service as a groom.

Now the king had a favourite stallion and often came to the stables to see that all was well with it. And all *was* well with it, for the lad groomed it till its coat shone like satin, and fed it and exercised it till the muscles rippled under its satiny skin. But one day the king came to the stable with tears in his eyes.

'Ah, my dear stallion,' said he, 'so often you have carried me in peace and in war! But the day is soon coming when you will carry me no more.'

Then the lad up and spoke, 'Your majesty, I know your trouble and I can ease it.'

'You!' said the king, all astonished.

'Yes, I,' said the lad. 'I know that the troll, my former master, will kill you if you do not pay back the six bushels of gold you owe him. But, sire, *I* have six bushels of gold, and I will lend them to you, if when you go to pay the troll you will allow me to go with you and run ahead dressed as a clown. I shall certainly play some crazy tricks, but you may take my word for it that all will turn out well. And I know where your daughter is, and I give you my solemn word that I will get her back for you. No, I am not jesting,' said he. And he went and dug up the six bushels of gold and brought the gold to the king.

Then the king took heart. He didn't quite believe that the lad could rescue his daughter; but at any rate he had the gold, and he mounted his stallion and set out to pay his debt to the troll. The lad disguised himself as a clown, with a grinning mask and a fool's cap, and a parti-coloured coat and baggy trousers; and he went along with the king, riding on an ass. But when they drew

near to the troll's mound, he jumped off the ass, and gave it a hearty slap. The ass turned round and galloped home, and the lad ran on before the king, leaping and shouting and playing every silly trick he could think of.

So they came to the troll's dwelling – and what did they see? Where the huge grassy mound had been, there now stood a magnificent palace.

'Oh ho! Oh ho!' shouted the lad, 'Our troll has come up in the world!' And he stood on his head and clapped his heels together. Then he rushed to the palace and began smashing windows, and breaking in doors, and doing all the damage he could.

Out came the troll – he was roaring with rage. 'Who's going to pay for all this damage?' he bellowed. 'Do you think *you* are going to pay for it – you puny little king? *You* who can't even pay your old debts?'

'But I – I can pay my debts,' stammered the king. And he gave the troll the six bushels of gold.

The troll, who could scarcely believe his eyes, fetched a bushel measure, measured the gold, and found it was exactly right. So he gave the king back the bond which he had signed, and said, 'I shall want another six bushels of gold to pay for all this damage.'

But the king hadn't any money left – no, not a halfpenny.

'So!' roared the troll. 'Both you and your fool shall lose your heads, unless you can answer three questions I shall put to you.'

The king was trembling like a jelly, but the disguised lad (who was all this time throwing stones through the broken windows) swung round and said, 'Ask away, *I'll* answer your questions!'

'*You!*' shouted the troll.

'Yes, *I*,' said the lad, bold as brass. And he flung a big stone *plump* at the troll's nose.

The troll brushed away the stone as if it had been a fly, and said, 'Tell me, where is my daughter?'

'At the bottom of the sea,' answered the lad. 'But she is not your daughter.'

'Would you know her if you saw her?' roared the troll.

'Oh yes, bring her here,' said the lad.

The troll gave a whistle; and there came out of the castle a procession of maidens, dressed in white, with roses in their hair. One by one they filed past the lad, and every maiden was as like every other maiden as a reflection in a mirror, and every one was the image of the lad's dear princess.

The lad held his breath and kept his hands clenched to his sides, so often did his heart urge him to leap forward and cry out, 'This, this, *this* is she!' But at last came one who, as she passed him, put up her hand and smoothed back her hair, and the lad caught her by the arm and cried out, '*This* is the princess!'

The troll wasn't pleased. He scowled and growled. 'Well, I own you're right,' said he. 'But you won't answer my next question so easily. Where do I keep my heart?'

'In a mouse,' said the lad.

'Ah ha!' But there are millions of mice in the world,' said the troll. 'You must tell me *which* mouse, or your head will fly from your body.'

'Bring in your mice!' said the lad.

The troll gave a whistle, and immediately over the ground millions of mice came scampering. They ran past the lad one behind the other. Which mouse indeed? How was the lad to tell that? But by and by the princess, whose arm he still held, gave him a nudge; the lad stooped, picked up a little grey mouse, and said, 'This is the one!'

And didn't he give that mouse a pinch! The mouse gave a squeak, the troll gave a scream, 'Stop! stop, stop!' he screamed, 'It's my heart you're pinching!'

'Aye,' said the lad, 'and I'll do more than pinch. I'll kill this mouse as sure as I stand here, unless you do as I say.'

'What must I do?' wailed the troll.

'Set free all the animals and birds you keep shut up in your stable,' said the lad, giving the mouse another squeeze.

'It's done! It's done!' shrieked the troll. 'See for yourself!'

Then up out of the ground, running, leaping, bounding and flying, came bears, foxes, hares, rabbits, wolves, squirrels, deer, and flocks of every kind of bird, all joyfully making their way back into the forest. The air rang with the joyous songs of the birds, and the earth echoed with the patter, and clap-clap, and thud-thud of the animals' running feet. But the lad still held the mouse tight in his hand.

'Don't you know me, sir troll?' said he. And he took the mask off his face and laughed.

'You squeeze me too tight,' moaned the troll. 'You squeeze me too tight – and I never did you any harm!'

'Nay, for a troll I'll own you treated me well,' said the lad. 'But I'm not trusting you. I have your heart in my hand, and I'll keep it in my hand, until your little daughter, as you call her, is safely home. Give your 'little daughter' a horse now, you old rascal, and give me another, for we've a mind to bid you goodbye.'

'I don't know where there are any horses,' moaned the troll.

'Then we'll see what a little pinch will do,' said the lad. And he gave the mouse another squeeze.

The mouse squeaked, the troll shrieked. He clapped his great hands, and two splendid horses, saddled and bridled, came galloping out of the forest. The lad lifted the princess on to one horse, sprang on to the other, the king mounted his stallion, and they all rode off.

And when they had ridden a long, long way, and had reached the borders of the king's realm, the lad, who still held the mouse in his hand, dismounted, and set the little creature on the ground.

'Be off now, little rascal!' said he.

The mouse scampered away – but where it went, who knows? Certain it is that to whatever place it went, the troll followed it. And neither mouse nor troll was ever seen in that country again.

So then the lad married the princess.

And now this story has no more to tell.

13. Nils in the Forest

There was a poor man called Nils who took a sack and went into the forest to gather firewood. And when he had filled his sack, he sat down under a tree to eat the bread and cheese he had brought with him. Then there came hobbling towards him a tiny, tiny dwarf man with a long yellow beard.

The tiny dwarf man was dressed in rags, and he was holding out a shrivelled little hand and whimpering, 'Spare a coin for a poor old man! Spare a coin for a poor old man!'

'Bless me, old fellow!' says Nils, 'I haven't any coins! All the coins I earn, and they're few enough, go to buy food for my wife and children. But you're welcome to a share of my dinner.'

And he gave the little dwarf man half of his cheese, and half of his loaf, and a long drink from his bottle of ale.

The dwarf gobbled up the bread and cheese and drank down the ale – and then what did he do? He clapped his shrivelled little hands together, and vanished.

'Well!' says Nils. 'Well! Not even a thank you!'

And he got up, slung the sack of firewood over his shoulder, and turned to go home.

He hadn't taken many steps, when the tree branches began to toss and roar, and the leaves began to fall down in showers; and out from behind the trees strode a huge troll wife with a head as big as a barrel, and a body as big as a barn, and a voice like two pieces of iron clashed together.

'What are you doing in my forest?' shouted the troll wife.

'Just gathering a few sticks, please, ma'am,' said Nils. 'I thought no harm. I didn't know the forest belonged to you.'

'Well, it does,' said the troll wife. 'And now I'm going to eat you.'

Nils fell on his knees.

'Oh please, ma'am, oh no, ma'am! I have a wife and seven little children. If you eat me, they will starve!'

'You should have thought of that before,' shouted the troll wife. 'But things being as you say, I'll play a game with you. You may try and hide from me three times. If I find you once, you may try again. If I find you twice, you may try again. But if I find you the third time, it's into my pot you go!'

Then the troll wife gave a roar of laughter, and strode away among the trees.

What to do now? Nils was looking round for somewhere to hide, when all at once there was the little dwarf man standing at his side.

The little dwarf man had an axe over his shoulder.

'Never say die, Nils!' says he. 'I'll hide you all right!'

So he up with his axe and chopped a splinter out of a tree. Then he took Nils by the hand and pushed him inside the tree, put the splinter back in its place, and went off chuckling.

Well, he hadn't gone very far when he met the troll wife, stamping along carrying an axe.

'Where are *you* off to?' says the dwarf man to the troll wife.

'Aa–aw,' says she, 'going to fell a tree.'

And she went straight to the tree where Nils was hidden, cut it down, and dragged Nils out of it.

'That's once,' says she. 'Next time you must hide better.'

And she went off shouting with laughter.

Nils walked on into the forest. He was frightened. He was searching about for somewhere to hide, when there was the little dwarf man standing at his side again.

'Come along,' says the little dwarf man. 'We'll beat her yet!'

And he took Nils out of the forest to a place where there was a lake with reeds growing thick along its margin.

The little dwarf man broke a reed in two, and gave Nils a clap on the shoulder. Nils dwindled down to the size of a pin. The dwarf man pushed him inside one half of the hollow reed, stuck the reed together again, and put it back amongst its fellows on the margin of the lake. Then he went off chuckling.

By and by he met the troll wife, striding along with a big knife in her hand.

'Where might you be going, ma'am?' says the dwarf man.

'Aa–aw–off to cut reeds,' says she. And she went down to the lake.

Chop, chop, chop. She cut down all the reeds.

Then she gathered up the reeds in her great hand, and shook them.

Shake, shake, shake : out from one reed fell Nils.

'That's twice,' says she. 'You must hide yourself better next time. My pot's on the boil.'

And she went off, shouting with laughter.

Nils's teeth were chattering. He thought of his poor wife and his seven little children, and no one left to work for them and earn them a bite of bread.

But the little dwarf man was at his side, and the dwarf man said, 'Cheer up, Nils, we'll beat her yet!'

He snapped his fingers. There now in his hand was a fishing rod baited with a fat worm. He cast his line: he caught a big fish. He broke the fish in half, put Nils inside it, clapped the two halves together again, and threw the fish back into the lake.

'Swim away, my fish!' said the little dwarf man.

The fish wriggled its tail and swam away.

The dwarf man went back into the forest. He was laughing. But in the forest he met the troll wife. She was carrying a wash tub on her back and a fishing net over one shoulder.

'Where are you off to with that wash tub?' says the dwarf.

'Aa–aw – down to the lake to catch fish,' says she.

And down to the lake she went, put the wash tub in the water, got into it, pushed off from shore, and cast her net.

'I'll be catching a big fish with something inside it presently,' says she.

But the dwarf man stood on the edge of the lake. He blew one mighty breath, a second mighty breath, a third mighty breath. Then arose such a storm as never was in the world before. The wind howled and beat upon the water; the waters of the lake rose up in huge waves. The waves dashed against the shore with such violence that the foam spurted up to the top of the trees in the forest. The wash tub was whirled this way and that way; the troll wife clung to the sides of the tub and screamed for mercy.

But the dwarf said, 'If you have ever shown mercy in your life, then mercy shall be shown to you; if not – down with you under the water.'

And with that the wash tub turned upside down: the troll wife sank to the bottom of the lake, and never more came up.

Then the dwarf man ceased to blow with his breath, and the lake became quiet. The dwarf man cast his line and caught the big fish.

He opened the fish, took Nils out of it, put the fish together again, and threw it back into the water.

'Goodbye, my fish. Swim away, my fish!'

The fish wriggled its tail, and swam away.

'The troll wife won't trouble us again,' said the dwarf man to Nils. 'Now come with me.'

He took Nils to a cave in the forest. The cave was the home of the troll wife, and it was stacked full of gold.

'All this gold is yours,' said the dwarf man to Nils. 'Fill your pockets and off home with you. Toworrow you can come with a horse and cart and fetch the rest of the treasure. . . . And thank you for the bread and cheese – and the ale,' says he, and clapped his wizened little hands together, and vanished.

Nils went home with his pockets full of gold. Next day he hired a horse and cart and came back to the cave for the rest of the treasure.

Now he was rich. He bought a big farm and prospered. He never saw the little dwarf man again; but he never forgot to say a 'thank you' to him every night and every morning. And sometimes he fancied he heard the dwarf man laughing. Maybe he did, maybe he didn't. Who can tell?

But one thing is certain: Nils and his wife and children lived richly and happily to the end of their days.